STEEL HEARTS

Copyright © 2021 by Ashlea Thompson

First Printing, 2021

Published using IngramSpark

Print ISBN 978-1-0879-7266-4
Ebook ISBN 978-1-0879-7267-1

Steel Hearts

ASHLEA THOMPSON

Ashlea Thompson Publishing

For my husband, who is always up for my crazy adventures.
And my Beau and Bama, my most precious fur babies.

~ 1 ~

Living in Birmingham is such a big difference from my hometown. Thomasville is a small town with one red light and a Square. Charming to most, but hell to me. Nothing to do, nowhere to go. I hated working on the farm. All I wanted to do was study Art and get out of town. So, I worked hard and got away. Sure, my parents were sad, but they knew I wanted something bigger. I didn't want the life my sister had. Samantha was the blonde tall flamboyant life of the party. The baby of the family and spoiled. She was Homecoming Queen and star cheerleader. To me, she was a cliché. She ended up at the University of Alabama on scholarship and was a cheerleader.

After I graduated from Montevallo, I found a job working at a gallery for local artists. I loved everything about it. It didn't pay much, so I worked another job as a waitress. I had to pay the bills somehow. Over the ten years I lived here, I finally felt free. Don't get me wrong. I didn't mind helping Daddy, but like I said I wanted something more.

Not much of a looker but pretty in my own way, I am 5 feet tall with long brown hair. I have tattoos (against my Daddy's wishes). Daddy called me his blue-eyed baby. My nose was always stuck in a book, and I was always studying. Even though I was the older of us two sisters, I always felt like Daddy was proud of me. "I was hoping you would carry on with the tradition of the farm. God knows I don't trust your sister," he said, rolling his eyes. "But I want you to know how proud I am of you. You have such a free spirit. You will always be my little girl." Daddy and Momma cried tears of joy on the day of my college graduation. I had been back home as much as I could. I loved them and missed them. They knew it was time for me to stand on my own. So, I did.

My love life was pretty much non-existent. I dated here and there, but they never really amounted to anything. In my spare time, I would go out with friends, or visit museums, or enjoy the day at a park. I would paint as well. I honestly didn't have a lot of spare time, but when I did, I treasured those moments. Then Jake Samford came along.

Jake Samford was a gorgeous six-foot-tall work of art. His green eyes would mesmerize you, and make you forget what you were saying or doing. He had sandy blonde hair. He comes from a wealthy family who owns Samford Steel Enterprises, LLC. I learned that he was now a partner of the business alongside his father, William Samford. His mother, Marie Samford, was well known throughout the area for her work with various charities and boards she sat on. My friends called them the perfect family. It made me want to gag.

Jake and his family came into the steakhouse I worked at for dinner one night. "Heads up chick, the Samfords are seated in your section," Amanda said, suggestively raising her eyebrows. "Don't you have work to do, chick?" I quipped back, rolling my eyes at her. She sneered at me and walked to tend to her tables. I waited a moment to collect myself before I went over. Everyone thinks they are a difficult family to serve. They always want the best. You had to work hard if you wanted a big fat tip. I never met the family in person, and this was the first time they sat in my section. For whatever reason, it made my anxiety stand on edge.

After they were seated, I sauntered up to their table. "Hi, welcome to Walter's. My name is Lottie and I will be your server. What can I get you to drink?" The words just rolled off my tongue easily enough despite the heat I felt rising in my face. Mr. and Mrs. Samford ordered the most expensive bottle of wine. It was $80 a bottle. My eyes almost bugged out of my sockets. I was able to keep calm, and by the time I got to Jake, he was giving me a big goofy grin. "And for you sir?" I asked, only slightly able to keep from stuttering. He was not someone I would find myself attracted to, yet here I was with butterflies in my stomach. "I will have a Maker's Mark on the rocks please," he replied, smiling from ear to ear. As I was walking to the bar, Amanda was staring at me with a shit-eating grin on her face. I shook my head and went to put in their orders.

After what seemed like an eternity, the Samford's were done with their meal. After settling the check, they started making their way out the door. Jake excused himself to the restroom. I turned around from the waitress station to go check on my tables and nearly ran into Jake. There he was standing in all his gorgeous glory. "Oh, I'm sorry. I didn't see you there," I said. "No, it's ok. I wanted to introduce myself.

I'm Jake. I didn't catch your name at the table," he said, smiling. Of course, he didn't. I was probably talking too fast. Possibly even stuttering. "My name is Lottie. Nice to meet you," I say. He smiles that grin from ear to ear. "That's a unique name, " he says, sticking his hand out to shake my hand. I hesitate but I shake his hand. His hands are strong. I stand there gaping at him. It's awkward. After a second, he says "Can I have your number? I would like to take you out for a drink sometime." He is quick and to the point. I see Amanda over Jake's shoulder staring with her mouth open. I give her a knock-it-off look. She finally nods in approval. "Uh, sure," I say. I write my number on a piece of receipt paper and hand it over to Jake. He smiles and says "Great. I will give you a call. Hope you have a good rest of your night, beautiful." He moves toward the door. I'm standing frozen with disbelief. What did I just do? I am mortified. Even more so knowing that he is not my type, not that I have a type. Why would a gorgeous man like Jake be interested in me? I am a short average brown hair woman covered in tattoos. He looks like he fell off an underwear billboard. Amanda races over. "Oh my God, Lottie. You lucky son of a gun," she says.

Closer to closing time, we start to clear our sections and tidy them up. Amanda and I haven't said a word to each other. We work diligently so we can leave on time. As we are walking towards our cars, Amanda stops and turns to me. "Do you think he will call?" she asks. "I have no idea. I wouldn't be surprised if he didn't. I'm quite sure he probably has a million women at his beck and call," I say as I reach my car.

The drive home isn't a long one, but tonight it felt like the longest drive I have ever taken. I keep going over the night in my head. How Jake would blush every time I came to the table. That goofy smile of his. The thought of him being interested in me made me laugh. It also made me excited. I didn't expect a phone call. I honestly thought I would never hear from him.

I finally made it home. I brush my teeth and change. I don't even bother taking off my makeup. I hate wearing it honestly. I'm just too tired at this point. I fall asleep immediately as my head hits my pillow.

It's 7 A.M. and my alarm clock is screaming. I wave my hand around searching for the vile thing, knocking stuff off my bedside. I don't have to be at the Gallery until 10 o'clock. I am exhausted from last night. We were so busy. I turn off the alarm clock and stick my head back under the blankets. I snooze for another thirty minutes. I hear my phone ping with a message. I finally open my eyes and roll over. I grab my phone and look at it with half-closed eyes. When I see who it's from, I shoot straight up in my bed. "Holy shit," I mutter to myself while I stare at the screen.

Jake: Good morning, beautiful.

My hands are shaking. I am shocked that he texted me. I managed to type a response.

L: Hi.

J: I would have called, but I'm in a meeting. How about lunch today?

I'm not even sure what to say. I haven't been out with anyone in a while. I made a point to stay out of the dating pool. I have been out with a few guys here and there. No one has piqued my interest. Mostly it was fun. I decided that I would give myself time to work on myself. Then when I was ready, I would find the right one.

L: Sure. 12? I am working at The Gallery today.

J: Send me the address. I will be there.

I got ready for work and gave Amanda a call. She told me she would stop by work after she dropped her son off at preschool. Her son is five. His name is Nate, and he is a handful. I love him just as much as I love Amanda.

I hang up the phone and unlock the door to The Gallery. It is not very big but a nice space in downtown Five Points. I love working here. The owner of the shop is Nina Tenney. She is 70 years old but loves Art. She is a painter herself and often has her art here on display. The Gallery also highlights local artists. She once told me that she was wary of hiring a young adult fresh out of college, but she saw great things in me. I have worked here for nine years. She kind of took me under her wing and taught me everything she knows. She is kind of my second grandmother.

I am working in the backroom when I hear Amanda rush through the door calling for me. I can tell that she has a lot of excitement in her voice. I just smile and shake my head as I make my way to the front. It's 11 o'clock. She hands me my coffee and says, "So tell me everything!" I roll my eyes. "There isn't anything, I mean he just texted me. That's all. He wants to take me to lunch." She narrows her eyes at me, thinking. "So, are you going to go?" she asks.

"I agreed to lunch. I have no idea why," I say. Amanda grins at me. Lord, what am I doing? We begin to talk about other things when Nina walks in. "What are you two birdies squawking about?" she asks. "A little bit of everything," I say. I shoot a warning glance at Amanda. She ignores it and proceeds to tell Nina my plans for lunch. I could kick her in the knee. Nina is looking at me and smiling. What is it with people smiling at me lately?

"Well my little bird, I never thought I would see the day," Nina says, patting my hand. Nina and Amanda start chit-chatting as I make myself busy. At ten 'til noon, the bell on the door rings as the door is opened. We all whip our heads toward the front of the Gallery. Jake is walking towards us with a bouquet of sunflowers and roses. Heat rises in my face. Nina whistles. All three of us are just standing gaping at this beautiful man. He is dressed in tight jeans, and a dress shirt the color of sky blue. It brings out his eyes, I clear my throat, "Um hi Jake."

"Hi ladies. Lottie. These are for you," he says, handing me the flowers. Nina and Amanda both have their mouths open in shock. They look like a couple of birds waiting to be fed. "This is my boss Ms. Nina Tenney and my best friend Amanda," I motion towards my friends. Each mutters a hello. "So nice to meet you both," Jake says, again with that smile of his. As I feel my face get hotter, Amanda reaches for the flowers, "I will just put these in a vase here. Nina, care to join me?" Nina slowly looks at Amanda then back to me. "Oh yes dear, let's leave these two alone. Enjoy your lunch little bird," she says. They both walk to the back.

"Little bird?" Jake asks with raised eyebrows. "Long story," I say. Jake smiles and takes my hand and walks me outside to the sidewalk. I hope we aren't going anywhere fancy, because honestly, I'm not dressed for it. I was certain he would not show up. Jake opens the door to his car, and I slide in. It is a sports car of course. I wouldn't expect anything less. "Do you like Indian food? I know this place is not far from here. It's a hole in the wall, but it is amazing food," he asks as he starts the engine up." I do. Those are the best kinds of places," I say. We don't speak much on the drive over, simply because I am too nervous to talk. There is old country music coming from the radio. I can't help but smile.

We reach the restaurant and park close to the door. Jake comes around and opens my door. I'm kind of shocked at this. I am not used to this either. I get out and we walk in. We are seated and place our orders. While waiting he is asking questions and we are making small talk. We sort of eat in silence. I notice that he cannot keep his eyes off me. I know my cheeks are flush. I cannot for the life of me stop blushing. We go through the usual questions. Life, job, school, hometown, etc. I am beginning to become more comfortable. "So why does Ms. Tenney call you little bird?" he asks. "When I started working at The Gallery, she sort of took me under her wing and taught me everything I needed to know that they didn't teach in college. That's what she started calling me, her little bird. She is like a second grandmother to me," I reply. "Well, looks like I'm going to be calling you Birdie," he says. First real meeting with him and I already have a nickname. I roll my eyes. It's my turn to ask a question. "Why did you ask me to lunch?"

He is putting the last bite of curry in his mouth, chewing with the thought, "Well, I have seen you working at Walter's. That was the first time you were our server. I've seen you working in other sections. Your smile is gorgeous. I haven't been able to take my eyes off you. And well, you are beautiful," he replies. Typical male I thought, I stifle a giggle. "I just worked up enough courage to talk to you." I roll my eyes again before I catch myself. He laughs with his belly. We finish lunch and take the long way back to The Gallery. I thanked him for lunch and walked in. Nina is sitting at her desk. She demands immediately I tell her how the lunch went. I have several texts from Amanda. Geez, she has no patience, but I love her anyway.

~ 2 ~

I haven't heard from Jake since we had lunch together. It's only been three days, but I still can't stop thinking about it. Why hasn't he called? Was I not what he thought? On a normal basis, I wouldn't even dwell on it. I would just chalk it up to the dating gods as a one-time thing. I keep telling myself it's no big deal. Part of me wishes he would though. I want to text him since I am not sure what he is doing, but I do not want to seem desperate.

It's my off day from The Gallery and Walter's. It is rare for me to have an off day from both places. There is so much I want to do today, but I don't want to. I clean my apartment and pay bills. I order pizza and lounge the rest of the afternoon and catch up on Netflix. I fell asleep at some point, with pizza sitting in my lap. My phone rings and I jump. I look at the screen and stare in horror as Jake's name flashes across. I finally pull myself together and answer before it goes to voicemail. "Hello?" I say. "Birdie! How are you?" he says. I can hear him smiling through the phone. "Well, hi." We go through the small talk and formalities. He tells me about his day, and how sorry he is for not calling 'til now. He says it's because he has been busy with work (sure, ok). He asks me what I have been up to and listens to me complain about work at Walter's. We have been on the phone for about an hour. I'm pretty sure this is out of character for me. I don't like talking on the phone. I am more of a texter.

"I would like to take you on a real date," Jake says after an awkward silence. I try to contain my excitement. "Sounds like a plan, Stan," I reply, trying to stay cool. I knock the phone on my forehead. Smooth there Lottie. "Ok, I will pick you up at 7," Jake replies with a laugh. I give him my address and we say our goodbyes. I have 4 hours to get ready. I am still for a moment, wrapping my head around the conversation. I snap out of it and call Amanda. "Girl I will be right over," she says with utter excitement. I end the call and go and shower.

Amanda rushes in with a makeup bag, several dresses, and Nate in tow. I despise dresses. I only own one. It's black. It is my wedding and funeral dress. After we settle Nate in front of the T.V. and snack, Amanda and I attempt to put me together for my date. I don't want to wear makeup, but Amanda convinces me to at least wear eye shadow. After she is done, we go through the clothes. We settle on a sundress patterned with sunflowers. It's not too dressy, in case we do something casual, but it's nice enough if we go to a fancy restaurant. "Heels or flats?" she asked me. "Um. Flats," I say. She narrows her eyes at me. "Heels are sexier. Plus, he is tall, it will give you height," she says. "Are you crazy! I don't want my first date to be to the ER. I will break my neck!" I yelled from the closet. I put my flats on and double-check myself in the mirror. I walk out into the living room. Nate turns around and looks at me. "Wow Aunt Lottie, you look pretty," he says shyly. My heart swells. I love that kid. "She sure does. Here let me fix your hair quick," Amanda says walking over to me. I decided to wear my hair down. It's not too hot outside so I know I won't burn up. My hair is thick. It's terrible in the summer.

After she is done fussing over me, she tells Nate it's time to go, and they ready themselves to leave. "Good luck tonight. Call me if you need me or if you want to get out of there quick," she says with a smile. I hug them both. Ten minutes later, I hear a knock at the door. When I open it, Jake is standing there, again with flowers. Roses and daisies this time. "Those are beautiful, thank you," I say, taking the bouquet. "Yeah they are, but they are nothing compared to you," he says smiling. Damn. He is smooth. I invite him in and he follows me to the kitchen. "This is a nice place you have here," he says as he looks around. It's not a big place. It is a one-bedroom apartment in the downtown area of Five Points. I like it though. He is wearing a polo shirt and jeans, with loafers. He looks handsome.

We leave after I put the flowers in a vase. When we reach the parking lot, I look for his sports car. Instead of driving the little sports car, he is driving a 1967 Ford Mustang. It is gorgeous. I am in awe. It was always one of my favorite cars. "You like it?" he asked me. "I love it. It's a beautiful car," I tell him while he opens the door. "Well, a beautiful car for a gorgeous woman," he replies. Damn he got me there. I blush and slide into the passenger seat. I imagine he has a car collection. It wouldn't surprise me to see him in a different car next time. If there is a next time. David Bowie is playing through the stereo, and he automatically gains brownie points.

We went to the movies, and we held hands. After the movie was over, we went for a walk. We discussed the movie and various other topics. We decided on a little Italian restaurant for dinner. The conversation was lite and easy to navigate. I was still so nervous but became more comfortable with the more time I spent with him.

After our dinner was done, we walked back to the car. It was a lovely night. Clear skies and more stars than I could count. We made it back to my place close to eleven. "Thank you for a lovely evening," I say as I unlock the door, "Would you like to come in for a few?" My stomach does a backflip when he says yes. I don't want this night to end, I have made a promise to myself to take this slow. I don't want to move fast. I haven't been dating anyone for a while. I am not used to it. I don't have any wine in the apartment or anything to drink other than tea and water. He agrees to a glass of sweet tea, and we sit on the couch. We continued our conversation from dinner. I am learning so much in one small period. He is easy to talk to. I am careful not to share too much since this is only our first real date. The lunch date the other day doesn't count.

After a few minutes of silence, he leans over and kisses me. Not a big kiss, but big enough to make my heart skip a beat. I close my eyes. When I open them, he is smiling at me. He bites his lip and leans back in. His kiss is intense. My brain is screaming NO NO NO. The rest of my body is screaming YES

YES YES. I'm not even sure what I am doing. I tell myself not to freak out, just go with the flow. Kissing turns into making out. He seems really into me, that maybe this is not just a one-night stand, I push away the panic. "I want you. Right now," he says breathlessly I nod my head and he takes my hand, leading me into the bedroom.

Pushing me down on the bed, he is kissing my neck. He raises and removes his shirt. Holy shit at his six-pack. I reach up and run my hands down his chest. "Let's get you out of this dress," he says as he kisses me once more. He helps me stand and unzips my dress as he kisses my neck. I let the dress fall to my feet. Thank God I have on a girly bra and underwear (I silently thank God for Amanda). I turn around and face him. I feel exposed and shy. He sucks in a breath, "Gorgeous. Just. Damn." I start to blush, he smiles and takes my hand, and pushes me back down on the bed. He goes back to my neck, then works his way down my breasts. I try to keep from giggling and squirming. The more I can't hold it in, the more he does it. I feel his mouth on my skin, and the smile on his lips. I keep waiting to wake up from this dream. This can't be real. Knowing my luck, it's not.

When he is done ravishing me, he moves back toward my lips, and he is kissing me. "May I?" he asks, whispering in my ear. "Yes. Please," I reply. He enters me, slowly and tenderly. He picks up speed. After a while, we both reached our climax together and collapsed on the bed. I rest my head on his chest. He kisses me on the forehead. "Wow," he says. We both chuckle. We start talking about anything and everything. Pretty soon we both fell asleep tangled together under the blanket.

It's 8 o'clock by the time I wake up the next morning. I work tonight at Walter's, and since it's Sunday I know it's going to be super busy. Jake isn't in my bed, so I convince myself it was a dream. All of a sudden, I smell bacon being cooked. I walk barefooted to the kitchen pulling my robe on. Jake is in the kitchen, cooking breakfast. I raise my eyebrows. Am I still asleep? I pinch myself and realize this is not a dream. Jake turns around and puts the bacon on the plate. He smiles at me, "Good morning, Birdie!' he exclaims, "I hope you are hungry. I have to toast the bagels, other than that, breakfast is ready." I smile and sit at the table. "Do you do this for all your girlfriends?' I ask as he sets my plate and coffee down in front of me. He laughs and says, "Only for one in particular."

We both eat and talk and laugh together. This feels so nice. When finished, we clean the kitchen together. It kind of feels like we have been doing this our whole lives. It's weird. When the last dish is washed and put away, Jake gets dressed. We kiss and say our goodbyes. I fix myself another cup of coffee and lounge on the couch. I remember my phone and when I pick it up, I have several texts and missed calls from Amanda.

A: How is the date going?

A: Did you make it home?

A: HEY!

A: HELLO. ARE YOU ALIVE?

A: OMG Answer your phone.

A: I'm about to put out a search party.

I snort and dial her number. "I was close to barging through your door," she says. "Don't be so dramatic Amanda, I'm fine," I say with a sigh. She wants all the juicy details and bombards me with all sorts of questions. I tell her everything she wants to know. By the time I am done, I need to get ready for work. I am working the early shift, so I end the call as quickly as I can. I get ready and pull in to work with 2 minutes to spare. As predicted, the night is super busy, and I am worn out by the time I get home. I take my shoes off before I open the door. My feet are swollen and are hurting. I open the door, and I am greeted by a room full of sunflowers. "Am I dead?" I ask myself as I step out into the hallway, looking down both ends of the hallway. There is a note on the coffee table:

A GORGEOUS WOMAN SHOULD BE SURROUNDED BY BEAUTI-FUL THINGS - Jake

My heart does that skipping thing it's been doing since I met Jake. I snap a picture and send it to Amanda. She sends back heart emojis. I change and get ready for bed. I lay there for a bit, unable to think because my mind will not shut off. Jake is all I seem to think about. My phone rings and it's Jake. He says he can't stop thinking about me, and we make plans to spend time together in the next few days. I finally fell asleep after an hour or so of hanging up with him. This is just too good to be true.

~ 3 ~

Over the next few months, Jake and I have been pretty much joined at the hip. He formally met Amanda and Nate and loves them as much as I do. He even offered to take Nate to the zoo, which in Nate's eyes, earned him best buddy status. Nina and Jake get along fine, and he helps her with the stuff around the gallery that she calls 'Man Tasks'. We take turns staying at each other's place. His home is in a quiet neighborhood in Homewood, and his house is gorgeous. I must admit I spend more time there than my apartment.

We are enjoying a quiet lunch at the deli a block from The Gallery. After a few minutes of silence, he looks at me and smiles. I'm mid-bite when he says, "I would like you to meet my parents. "I kind of gasp and end up almost choking. "I'm sorry, what?" I manage to say after I swallow my bite, "I want you to meet my parents. I want to meet your parents too. Maybe we can all have dinner together," he says, trying not to laugh. He gauges my reaction. I think about my mom and dad. They would be fish out of water. I smile. "Sure," I say,

We figure out when and where, and I make the phone call to my parents. They are excited and happily agree. I have knots in my stomach, and I pray it all goes well. They aren't exactly country bumpkins, but they are as country as they come. A week later, we all met at Fleming's Steak House for dinner. It went smooth for the most part. Jake asked all about the farm and Jake's parents are wonderful and welcoming. It's not the disaster I thought it was going to be. My heart is happy. Jake reaches over and squeezes my hand. This is a breeze to him. I've been a nervous wreck. The next day I see my parents off as they travel back to Thomasville. I text Jake, and then I get ready to go to work. Nina is all ears. I tell her about dinner. Amanda stops by and Nina fills her in while I help a customer.

Two days later, we met for dinner before my shift at Walter's. Jake is so giddy and happy. His mother told me that he has never felt this way about anyone. I'm not quite sure what she meant by that, so I kind of let it pass by without dwelling on it. He walks me to my car and gives me a big bear hug. "My you are in a chipper mood today," I say as I struggle for him to put me down. "Oh, I am. And let me tell you why," he says. He kisses each cheek and my forehead and gives valid points, I'm beautiful, I'm gorgeous, and I am fun. I snort. Then, as he reaches my lips, he says, "And I love you."

My heart does that skippy thing again (I need to get that checked) and I look at him. He is staring at me anxiously. "Really?" I ask finally. "Yes, I do. I love you," he says while he blushes. "I love you, too," I say finally. He kisses me, then kisses my forehead. "Good. Now, go to work," he says as he opens my door, and I slide into my car. I am on cloud nine. Things are going well, and I can't wait to tell Amanda, I grab my phone and shoot her a quick text. The next day he asks me to move in with him. I ask him if I can give it some thought. This is all happening so fast.

Amanda and I have taken Nate to the park. It's a nice day. Spring is just now starting to arrive, and we all know about Alabama weather. So, we take advantage. I watch Nate running around and sliding down the slide. He is so happy and watching Amanda swell up with pride makes my heart swell. They are family to me. "So, I have some big news," I say. Amanda takes a sip of her tea, and says, "Do tell."

I tell her about Jake and the big L and him wanting me to move in with him. She stays silent and nods at the right parts. For a moment she stays quiet. After a few minutes, she looks at me and says, "Is this what you want? This is all so fast and sudden. You guys haven't been together long. Do you have a backup plan?" She is right. I am the kind of person that weighs out the options and cautiously decides. Amanda, forever the mother hen. "When you know, you know," I say. I run to Nate and we play and swing and slide.

I think a lot about what Amanda said when I told her that we were moving in with each other. I'm having fun. I feel like I have found the one person I want to spend the rest of my days with. We may not come from the same background. I know we are complete opposites. What is the saying? Do opposites attract? I like to think about what we lack in some areas we make up for in the others. Sure, the money is nice, but it's not what makes me so attracted and in love with him. He is kind and courteous. He helps people where he can. I am so far out of my comfort zone. It feels good though, and I try not to dwell on what ifs.

I have never lived with anyone other than my parents. I have always lived alone when I moved to Birmingham. I am anxious and excited. Of course, my conscience is screaming at me, but in the end, I think I have made a good choice. After a day or so, I tell Jake that I will move in with him. He arranges everything. The next week with the help of Amanda and Jake, I packed my apartment up. Jake tells me not to worry about anything because he will take care of everything. I quit my job at Walter's. I keep my job at The Gallery. I love Nina too much to leave her high and dry.

Jake's home is so pretty. It is a brick home with two stories, four bedrooms, two baths, a three-car garage, and a pool. It is spacious and open downstairs. Never in my life have I ever seen something like this. The house I grew up in was an old farmhouse that my parents renovated. But this home puts that home to shame.

When I am not working at The Gallery, I spend time by the pool, or in Jake's study reading. Amanda brings Nate to swim. Sometimes they come over for dinner. Nina comes over for dinner and swims, too. I love seeing her happy. Jake and I go on getaways and shopping. We spend time at home curled up on the couch. It's heaven.

Since Jake is working late, I go have dinner with Amanda and her family. Nina comes, too. Nate adores her. It's been a wonderful evening. I get a text from Jake:

J: Where are you?

L: At Amanda's.

J: Why?

L: You were working late. I came over here for supper.

J: You need to come home.

I excuse myself from the table and step outside. I called Jake, "What is wrong?" "I don't understand why you can't be home when I get home. You are always off doing something," he says, "You didn't call or tell me or anything. When I'm home, so are you, got it?" I look at the phone. Who does he think he is talking to? "Well, let me finish here, and I will head home," I say. "No. Home. Now." he says and hangs up on me. I'm so shocked. What the hell has gotten into him. I let Amanda know what's going on. I apologize and leave.

Jake's mood is a little lighter as the night wears down. I'm not even sure what's going on. I don't want to fight so I leave it alone. I apologize and tell him it won't happen again. He has been on and off his phone. I end up sitting on the couch watching a movie alone.

~ 4 ~

Things have been better since Jake's outburst. Even though he hasn't apologized, and I haven't pushed the issue, he seems in a better mood lately. It is Jake's Birthday week, and we go to Gatlinburg for the entire week. I am stoked because I haven't been since I was a kid. The Samford's own a cabin (shocker) near Mt Leconte. It's a two-story log cabin, with a breathtaking view. When we arrive in the afternoon, we decide to stay in and enjoy the hot tub. We get up early the next morning, to drink coffee and watch the sunrise. Jake has to make some calls for work which makes me a little upset. Who works on vacation? I decided while he works, I will go shopping for his birthday gift.

I'm cruising down the Parkway when I pass an Adult Store. On an impulse, I pull into the parking lot. I hype myself to go in. "Hi sugar, Can I help you find something?" the lady at the counter asks. At this point, all I can do is stare at the floor. I know for a fact my face is the color of a tomato. "Yes, I am looking for something to wear for my boyfriend's birthday," I say awkwardly. "Honey I have just the thing for those curves of yours," the lady says. She leads me over to the clothes I decided to buy a black lace teddy. I want to start his

Birthday week off right. I work out a plan on the drive back to the cabin.

Jake is working out on the back porch. "Hey there Birdie, whatcha got in all those bags?" he asks, smiling ear to ear. "Oh, a little of this and that," I say. I tell him I am going upstairs to go through all my bounty. I kiss him on the forehead and climb the stairs. I decided to take a soaking bath. I take the lingerie out of the bag, and I snort at the thought of what I am about to do. I'm nervous too, but I'm hoping to take his attention away from work for a while and a little afternoon delight before dinner.

After the water grows cold, I get out of the tub. I blow-dry my hair. I decided not to wear make-up. I shimmy into the little black frock. I look in the mirror one last time. Damn, I'm looking pretty hot. I pad down the stairs, but I don't see Jake on the porch, he must be in the sunroom. I see him as I walk down the hallway to the back of the cabin. He is standing and it looks like he is talking to himself. I shake my head and grin. Before my courage disappears, I walk around the corner, "Oh honey, how about a little dessert before dinner?" Jake looks up with a surprised look, and he is blushing big time. When I finally register what the look on his face is, I look and see his parents sitting on the couch.

I am mortified and embarrassed. Jake rushes over and throws a blanket over me. "Mr. Samford. Mrs. Samford, I uh. Um..." as I nod to each of them. Mr. Samford stares at the floor, kind of chuckling to himself. The look on Mrs. Samford's is appalling. "I'm just going to go back upstairs now, and you know, drown myself in the toilet," I say and turn around and run back upstairs.

After a good fifteen minutes, Jake stands in the doorway. "They are gone now," he says. I look up at him still wrapped in the blanket with tears in my eyes. "I had no idea they were here. I'm so sorry," I say. "It's ok baby, they just came up to surprise me for my birthday. They are staying in town," He says as he walks over to me, "Now, how about that afternoon delight?"

We have dinner at The Greenbriar, a charming restaurant nestled in a little holler. Jake and his dad discuss the normal things, but Mrs. Samford remains quiet. She looks everywhere but at me. I try to make some conversation, but I am failing miserably. I'm beginning to think she doesn't like me. I keep quiet for the rest of the meal. Jake squeezes my hand. He knows my anxiety is high. We finish dinner, and Mrs. Samford wants photos taken. We go through the motions and then say our goodbyes. The following day, Jake and his parents go visit friends in the area, and I elect to stay at the cabin. I read most of the day and enjoy the sunshine out on the back deck. When Jake returns, he doesn't seem to be happy. His mood changes. I can't figure out what is wrong, but I don't worry too much about it. We spend the rest of the week exploring. We do all sorts of stuff. He takes me over to Cherokee, we gamble, I win. We went to Bryson City. It's such a charming little town. I almost do not want to go home.

The drive home is a quiet one. Jake doesn't say much. "Is everything ok?" I ask apprehensively. "Yeah Birdie, everything is fine," he says. He takes my hand and holds it the rest of the way home. I am pretty sure something is wrong, but I don't push it. I fell asleep for the rest of the trip. I'm exhausted.

~ 5 ~

I go visit Amanda and Nate. Nate is over the moon at the stuffed bear I brought him back. He is sitting in front of the tv and playing. I'm not much of a drinker, but Amanda insists on drinking some of the moonshine I brought her home. We talk about the trip, and I tell her about the misfortune of me trying to be sexy. We had a good laugh. Nate wants to go play outside, so we bask in the sun in her backyard.

"It's so weird. I thought everything was fine. He has just been distant the past few days," I say. "Do you think his parents said something to him?" She asks, thoughtfully. "I have no idea. I think it might be work stuff. He has been stressed with a new project he has been working on," I say, taking a sip of my drink, "I want to say something, but I don't know what to say. He hasn't been this way before with me." We sit in silence. Nate's imagination is on fire today, and he has been quite the Chatty Kathy. "I think it's because you guys are moving fast," Amanda says. I nod but don't say anything. I mean, He might be overwhelmed with everything. "I mean, it's only been what, 7 months?" she continues, "You guys are joined at the hip most of the time. It's kind of creepy." I know what she is trying to get at. The way I feel about Jake is unlike the way I have felt about anyone else. I just wing it most of the time. I am trying not to rush things. I just want to stay happy.

Things have gotten better over the next few months. We are approaching our first anniversary. Though I think celebrating such milestones is stupid, especially since I'm not that type of girl, I get excited. I am off today, and I plan to cook a feast of Jake's favorite food. I'm not much of a cook, I try though, so Amanda comes over to help. I want to spend a nice evening at home and since Jake has been working like a mad man, I want to make sure the evening is perfect, and he can relax. I bring some wine from the cellar (he has a freaking wine cellar) and set the table. Jake will be home in an hour, so I shoot him a quick text with a picture of the wine.

L: See you soon. Prepare yourself for the best feast of your life. XOXO.

J: :)

Ok, not the response I wanted but whatever. He is probably busy. I take a shower and dress in comfy clothes. When Jake gets home, he goes upstairs to change. "I have a nice relaxing night planned for us honey, with your favorite foods and all. I was thinking we could watch an old black and white movie," I say, smiling as I pour some wine. "Sounds good," he says. He has been scrolling on his phone since he got home. I think to myself WTF is going on here. I push my thoughts back and we start eating. The conversation is light. We talk about our day and such. Then there is an awkward silence.

I clear my throat, "Do you know what today is?" He looks at me puzzled. "No, he says." I kind of sit there, not knowing what is about to happen. "Today mark's one year of being together," I smile. He looks at me with a blank face. Ok, cool. "I didn't know. It's been that long?" he says, checking his phone. That damn phone, I could throw it in the yard. Jake gets up to go to the bathroom but leaves his phone. I look over at it and see he has a text message. I can't see the name, but the text says:

'Are you with her? You could be with me. I want you bad right now. Come on over and I will show you.'

"I thought you didn't care about such things," he says as he sits back down. To keep from saying something ugly, I quickly pop a meatball in my mouth and chew slowly. The rest of the meal is met with silence. When he is done, he goes to his study. I cleaned up the kitchen. I sit on the couch and finish the bottle of wine. What is happening? Is there someone else? Is he done with me? What has changed? I go over and over this in my mind. I have drunk a whole bottle of wine, so I feel courageous at this point. I knock on the door of his study.

He motions for me to come in, and I sit in the chair by the window. "Thank you for dinner. It was really good," he says as he sits the book he is reading down. I nod my head. After a few minutes, I looked over at him. I have a million thoughts running through my head. Before I can stop myself, I mumble, "You've been distant the past few weeks. What's wrong? Is it me?" Now I sound like a typical woman. I shake my head. When he finally looks at me, I am on edge. I'm holding my breath. "No," he says. I want to figure this out, but I don't want to seem like I am crazy.

"Then what is going on? You barely said two words to me at dinner," I managed to say. I get up and walk over to the couch where he is sitting. "I want a future with you. I've been thinking about it a lot here lately. I can't imagine myself with anyone else," I say.

"Why can't we just stay the way we are?"

"I want more."

"I'm not ready to settle down. I don't want a family. You have no idea what marriage is like and what it consists of. It's hard."

"How would you know; You have never been married."

He looks up at me with a blank face. I think I've hit a nerve. "Wait, you mean to tell me you've been married before?" I ask, feeling sick to my stomach. Normally it wouldn't be a big deal. Everyone has a past. Jake drops his head in his hands. "Why didn't you tell me?" I ask. He looks at me, he doesn't want to have this conversation. We are going to have it though. Rip the band-aid off. "It's irrelevant," he pops off.

"So, you hid it, you asked me all about my past. I told you. How is it irrelevant? If you neglected to tell me, then it makes me wonder what else you are hiding."

"She left me. Took everything I had. Cleaned me out. I had to build from the ground up. I worked hard for what I have now."

"This is bullshit."

"Lottie, please."

"Don't you Lottie me. I'm trying to tell you how I feel, and you drop this bomb on me."

"It doesn't matter."

"But it does."

"I like the way things are now. We are having fun. Don't ruin this. I love you, but I don't want more than what we have now. I just don't."

"Do you think I'm like her? I'm just going to take everything and run? We've been honest with each other so far. Why not say something. That's sort of a big deal." He picks up his phone. "Don't you dare," I say through clenched teeth.

"This is not a big deal. Let it go."

"Well, I think I'm done here then."

"What is that supposed to mean?"

"You aren't my favorite person right now," I say. I leave the study as tears are streaming down my face. I go upstairs and slam the door. Jake sleeps on the couch for the next few days. I am so hurt. Not only because I have given so much time to spend with him, but because I laid my heart bare to him, and he took a big shit on my heart. I can get over him being married once before, but I can't get over the fact that he didn't tell me.

I text Amanda and tell her what has happened. I know she is out with her husband tonight since her mom is keeping

Nate. She calls me the next morning. I agree to come over for a while. We talked about what happened while I helped her in her garden. Amanda has a way of giving tough love when I need it. She understands me. I need to decide. She is right. I decided the best thing for me is to break up with Jake. Since there is no future apparently, why stay? I don't want to be best buds or whatever. I'm not some friend with benefits either. The more I think about it, the more I have convinced myself that that's what this is. That night, I wrote a list of things I will need to do. Thank God I stored much of my stuff in a storage unit. I planned on going through it and getting rid of things I didn't need. Good thing I never got around to it. Now I just have to find another apartment. So, there is that.

~ 6 ~

While working at The Gallery the next day, I tell Nina everything that has happened. She knows some, but not all of it. "Honey, don't stress yourself out. Why don't you stay in my guest house? I won't charge you rent. Just help me around the house," she says. "Nina, that is so nice. I would love too," I say, hugging her. Nina is the most precious human being, I love her so much. She reminds me of my grandmother in so many ways. I made a phone call to my momma, and then to Amanda. Everything seems to be looking up, at least for now. I decided tonight I will tell Jake I'm leaving. I shoot him a text:

L: Will you be home tonight?

J: Of course. I miss you.

I roll my eyes and I leave the text unanswered. I finish up work and kiss Nina's cheek before leaving for the day. We've talked about the arrangements and when I will move in. She says she is excited to have a youngin' around the house again. She makes me laugh. Poor Nina. Since her husband died, and her kids moved out to start their own lives and family, it's just been her. Although she is spry in her old age, I feel better knowing I will be around to help her. Amanda says I can stay with her, but I think this will be much better. I have my own space, with a bathroom and a small kitchen. It's perfect.

I'm out on the back deck drinking a cup of tea and thinking about what all has happened. I try to do some reading but it's not helping me to keep my mind off the conversation I am about to have with Jake. I consider some liquid courage but decide against it. I want a clear mind. I want to mean what I say to him, even if it hurts. It is crazy to think about the past year. I thought we were golden. I've been thrown for a loop. I know there is nothing here for me, this relationship is a dead end. That's exactly what it is.

I hear Jake pull into the garage and come through the kitchen. My heart is in my throat. I am so nervous because I have no idea how this will go. I'm not a fan of confrontation. I will not let him get to me. I have made the decision and I am going to stick with it. "I thought I would find you out here. It's a beautiful afternoon," he says. He sits down in the rocking chair next to me, "Jake, we need to talk," I say matter of factly. "Ok, what's up?" he asks. "I am leaving. I can't stay in this relationship. You made it clear to me that there is no future," I say, swallowing hard.

He reaches for my hand, but I don't take it. "What do you mean?" he asks me, the color has drained from his face.

"I mean I am moving out. You told me that you like the way things are. It's like we are friends with benefits, I feel more like a roommate with perks."

"But I love you."

"Not the way that I have loved you. I want a family, Jake. I wanted to spend the rest of my days with you. But you don't want that. You just want to parade me around town like some sort of trophy. I am not a trophy."

"Lottie please don't do this," he says, voice cracking. "This is the choice I am making, I'm sorry. I will move my things out within the next week." Jake is looking at me like I just told him his cat died. He has tears streaming down his face. I feel bad, but I have to do this. I have to do this for myself. He needs to understand that. The sun is setting so I make my way inside. He follows me, asking me why and what he can do to make me stay. There isn't anything to make me stay. He doesn't want a future with me, so why do it when it's not what he wants. "I am going to stay with Amanda. I will be back tomorrow to start packing, I am going to bed," I say. He doesn't follow me upstairs. I lay awake most of the night. I am proud of myself for standing my ground and not giving into him. I've noticed that he is used to getting what he wants. Well not this time and certainly not with me.

Since I can't sleep, I go down to the kitchen to make myself a cup of tea. Jake is asleep on the couch. Judging by the empty whiskey bottle, he has been drinking and he is dead to the world, so I don't worry about waking him up. I grab my mug of tea and start back to the stairs when I hear his phone ping with notifications. I try to ignore it, but it's two o'clock in the morning for Christ's sake. Curiosity gets the best of me. I tiptoe over and grab his phone, and I go back into the kitchen. I can still see Jake, and I keep my eye on him even though I know he won't wake up.

I am not a person that snoops. I find the usual. Work stuff and such. Next, I take a look at his text messages. My stomach knots at what I find. There are several text messages from a woman called Sarah. I read through the messages. My eye is twitching. I cannot believe this. The filth. It seems as though he wants his cake and to eat it too. I take screenshots (for proof), and I set the phone back on the coffee table. I go back upstairs and pack a bag. It's too early in the morning to call Amanda or Nina, so I drive around trying to process everything. Here is this man, who swears he loves me and would do anything for me, yet he is out whoring around. I am angry, hurt, and betrayed. How can he want things to stay the way they are when he is interested in another woman? This solidifies my leaving.

By 7 am, I'm starving. I stop at a small dinner for breakfast. I got a text from Jake.

J: Where are you?

L: None of your business.

I text Amanda, and I drive to her house. She opens the door as I pull in, I haven't told her what has happened. She wraps her arm around me, and the tears start flowing. I call Nina, and she understands. She tells me not to worry about anything. She insists on me taking the day off. I take a shower. When I lay down, I pass out. I sleep hard for the next eight hours.

I do my best to keep Nate occupied while Amanda cooks dinner. "I knew he was no good," Amanda says while she is stirring the spaghetti sauce. "Elaborate," I say, coloring with Nate. "I mean, he is rich, comes from a wealthy family. He has everything he could want. He is an only child. I would bet every dollar I ever made that he is a Momma's boy," Amanda shrugs while pouring noodles into a strainer. Amanda starts listing other reasons. I think about the first time I heard about Jake and the Samfords. They are a prestigious family with a very successful steel company. Some would consider him the most eligible bachelor. Well 'til I came along, I guess.

~ 7 ~

I want to confront Jake about what I found on his phone. Amanda and Nina both say that I should just leave it alone. This hurts too much, and I want answers. I go back to the house with plans of starting to pack what I have there. It's not much. It will probably just fill a few boxes. I don't need any help, but Amanda offers me company. I decline. It's just something I need to do on my own.

Jake hasn't answered any of my calls or texts all day. When I am done packing, I try to call him one more time. It goes straight to voicemail. Of course, it does. I wonder if I should stay here 'til he gets home, or should I go to his office. I would much rather have this conversation in private, but if I have to, I will do it in front of God and everyone.

L: I need to talk to you. Please answer me.

J: I'm busy.

Yeah right. He is trying to avoid me because I believe he knows that I figured out what is going on. I load my car and take my stuff to Nina's. I stop at the store to get what Nina needs since she is sick. I am starting to worry about her. I'm glad I decided to stay with her. After I drop everything off, I head to Samford Steel. I sit in the parking deck, going over what I am going to say. I have it worked out in my head. I tell myself to remain calm and civil. I have no idea how this is going to go. If this is what he wants, then I'm going to give it to him.

I have been here several times before. I walk through the atrium, stopping to chit-chat with everyone. I finally make it to the elevator after what seems like a lifetime of hearing about Mrs. Nelson's cat. My heart is starting to race as I try to keep calm. I put the key to his house and the screenshots of his texts to Sarah in an envelope. It feels heavy in my hand. When I walk off the elevator, the receptionist greets me with a smile, "Good afternoon Lottie, what can I do for you?"

"I'm here to see Jake, dear. Just tell him he has a visitor," I say. She asks me to take a seat and to wait a moment. Usually, I would just walk to his office, but I don't want him to know I'm coming. The receptionist has been gone longer than I think she should. I stand up and start to walk towards Jake's office. The receptionist rushes up to stop me. That's when I see Jake. He is standing at what I assume is his assistant's desk. The woman sitting there is a blonde woman. She is gorgeous. I can see her blue eyes from where I'm standing. She is smiling and giggling. Jake is doing the same. I can't hear their conversation, but I am pretty sure they are flirting. I think that this is Sarah. I could be wrong. I walk briskly over, "Jake."

He jumps and turns and sees me standing there. The blonde has stopped talking, and her cheeks turn red. "What are you doing here?" he asks, with shock on his face. "Well, you won't return my calls or texts so, I had no choice," I say matter of factly, "And who is this?" Jake looks at me then back at the woman. "This is my assistant Sarah. Sarah, this is Lottie, my girlfriend," he says. "Ex-girlfriend," I say as I shake her hand. "Did you know he had a girlfriend, or did you not just care?" I ask her. Jake is mortified. He quickly ushers me into his office, shuts the door, and pulls the blinds closed. "What the hell is your problem?" He says to me, as he is pacing the floor. I sit down on the couch. I am holding the envelope in my hands. "My problem is that you have ignored my calls and texts for the past two days. I've been trying to talk to you, and you have avoided me. The only way I knew to get through to you was to come here. And I see you have been peacocking already. Well really, you've been doing it for a while now," I say in a snarky tone.

"What is that supposed to mean?"

"You know you ask that question a lot. Let me lay it out for you. I'm leaving you. You stated yourself that there is no future here. You don't want to settle down or have a family. You also kept from me that you had previously been married. I have come to realize that it doesn't matter that you were. The fact is you kept it from me. I would have been fine either way, but you didn't give me a chance to show you. It makes me think that there is other stuff that you keep from me," I say as I nod at the door.

"I was going to stay, even though you don't want the same things I do, I was willing to stay because I love you," I say, after I hand him the envelope, "The key to your house is in there. Have a nice life." I don't wait till he opens the envelope. I proceed past Sarah's desk, "Good luck. He will never want anything other than what you are giving him right now." I press the button on the elevator and step in. I could have been violent. I could have punched both of them. I am pretty proud of the way I handled things. By now, he has probably opened the envelope with the damning evidence of his infidelities. That's the last time I see Jake Samford.

"I don't know why you stayed as long as you did," Amanda says, unpacking a box of coffee cups. Nina is sitting on the couch, supervising, "Oh hush child, the heart will do what the heart wants." All three of us are a hoot together. My heart is happy to be able to spend time with them now that Jake is not in the picture. We spend the rest of the afternoon unpacking all of my stuff, talking shit about anything and everything. Nina walks back to the house to get us some iced tea. "Have you noticed anything weird going on with Nina?" I ask. Amanda looks at me, "Not really, I mean she is a bit forgetful. She called me her daughter's name the other day and asked me how my dog was. We don't even have a dog." This causes me to let out a small chuckle. I have noticed that Nina has been a bit off here lately. She has been sick off and on for the past month and a half.

~ 8 ~

After about three months of living in the guest house, I moved into the big house with Nina. One day, Nina was cooking breakfast. She was cooking bacon and walked off. I was sitting on the porch drinking coffee when I heard the fire alarm. I raced into the kitchen and put the fire out. I found Nina in the living room confused. She had no idea where she was. Yesterday, I got a call from the police, saying they found her wandering down the street, again confused. According to the officer, she was talking all sorts of nonsense.

I made a phone call to her son, Derrick. I told him I had concerns about his mother. We made a plan to get her to the doctor. I told him that I would take care of her. That he had nothing to worry about. I had an uncle that had Alzheimer's. I was familiar with it. She is having signs that she may have developed the disease. Derrick and I agree on this. A few days later, I was able to get her to her doctor. They run all sorts of tests. She is not a happy camper. The bad days are terrible. The good days are few and far between. I call Amanda while Nina naps, "I'm so lost. I have no idea what to do. I can't leave Nina at home by herself. I can't get any work done at the

Gallery. Her son and daughter want her in a nursing home. Nina refuses."

"Maybe try to catch her on a good day when she is lucid. Talk to her about it. She may have to close the gallery," Amanda says. That makes me sad. That gallery is her pride and joy. I try to think of ways that we can avoid that. To be honest though, The Gallery hasn't been doing well, and it has been losing money. "At this point, I think that may be the only option we have. Nina is a full-time job now," I say, "It's getting worse every day." We finish our call, and I finish fixing tea for Nina and me. I walk slowly down the hall to the living room, careful not to drop the tray.

Nina isn't in the living room where I left her. I set the tray down and call her name. When I do not get a response, I start searching the house. I know I locked the doors, so she has to be somewhere in this house. I make a loop around the house. When I reach the kitchen again, I see Nina laying on the ground. "Oh my God!" I scream and rush to her side. She is unresponsive, I can't tell if she is breathing or not. I run and grab the phone and dial 911. I start chest compressions and follow the dispatcher's instructions. My face is hot and soaked with tears. This is all my fault for not watching her. When the paramedics arrive, they take over. I'm sobbing hard at this point. I rode in the ambulance with Nina. She doesn't look good. The paramedics think she may have had a stroke.

I rushed to the waiting room. My hands are shaking as I make the call to her son. It was one of the hardest phone calls to make. He says it will be a few days before he and his sister can make it down. I tell him that's ok and I will update him with any news I hear. Amanda has come to sit with me. "Everything is going to be ok. She is strong," she says, pulling me in for a hug. We've been sitting here for three hours. Not one person has come to talk to us. When Derrick calls for an update, I tell him I haven't heard anything, and I will call him as soon as possible. I pace the waiting room. Finally, about an hour later, the doctor comes in. It looks like the news isn't good. Are you Nina Tenney's family?" The doctor asks. "Yes, I'm Lottie," I walked over to him.

"Mrs. Tenney suffered a major stroke. She also experienced a mild heart attack. We also noticed some pneumonia setting up in one of her lungs. The prognosis is not good. Has she shown any signs of a stroke or heart attack?"

"Not that I am aware of. I have been her caregiver for the past few months. She was diagnosed with Alzheimer's about a month ago. The doctor says he was pretty much healthy other than that."

"Sometimes, these things can come on quickly. Sometimes it is slow. Right now, she is on a vent. We need to speak to one of her immediate family members. She is on a ventilator and is in the ICU. We will let you back to see her when the next round of visitation starts, should be in about an hour."

I give the doctor Derrick's number. I text Derrick to let him know to expect a call from the doctor. Amanda leaves to pick up Nate. I am by myself in the waiting room. My heart is heavy, and I don't know what is going to happen. When I walk into her room, I am overcome with emotions. She is hooked up to monitors and has tubes and lines going every which way. How did she get so sick so quickly? She hasn't felt well the past two days, but then again, it's hard to tell with her. I sit next to her bed and hold her hand. I can't seem to stop the tears from falling. I kiss her cheek and tell her that everything is going to be ok. I leave when visiting hours are over. I go back home. I make some tea and call Derrick. He has been very kind and helpful over the past months when it has come to Nina. Both he and his sister have come to visit at least once. They both plan on coming down in the next few days. I finally fell asleep around midnight, It's the worst sleep ever. I keep tossing and turning.

Her daughter, son, and their families came down two days later. I moved back into the guest house because there is more room in the big house for them. I feel like everything is falling apart. I call my momma. Through sobbing and being choked up, I tell her everything. "Oh, my little chicken, you have to go through the storm sometimes. I know this is all very hard. You will make it through. I promise," she said. That makes me feel a little better but not by much. I finally got some much-needed sleep thanks to the bottle of wine I picked up on the way home from the hospital.

I have worked at the gallery all week. It has been unusually busy this week. I'm not complaining. I keep busy with cleaning and putting out new things. I want to keep my mind busy since I don't want a breakdown, especially if a customer comes in. I have ignored my phone pretty much all week. All I have done is go to work and come home. I like it that way. The only person I have talked to is my momma. Amanda checks in, but she knows how I deal with things. I tend to shut down. On the way home I get some take-out and make plans to catch up on my reading.

At about eight-thirty, there is a knock at my door. It's Derrick. "Hi, come in," I say as I open the door. He doesn't look so well. "I just thought I would stop by and tell you in person," he says, taking a seat. I get him a cup of tea and sit down on the couch opposite him. I have an idea of what he is about to tell me, but I don't interrupt him. "Mom has taken a turn for the worse," he says. I sit still for a moment, trying to ignore the lump in my chest.

"The doctors say that Mom is deteriorating quickly. Even though the machine is breathing for her, she is just sick. Her heart is not working as it should. Her kidneys are shutting down. Her lungs are weak. We have decided after a lot of thought, that we are going to make her a 'Do Not Resuscitate' and take her off the ventilation in the morning. I know this is hard to hear. I know you guys were close. We consider you family and would like for you to be with us" he says. I'm having a hard time comprehending all of this. I mean I know what it means. He lets me know what time they are going to the hospital tomorrow. I thank him and tell him I will be there.

I am up and ready. I followed the family to the hospital. We stand quietly around her hospital bed. I sort of stand to the side so that the family can be closer. No one speaks. After some time, the nurses come in along with Respiratory. The nurse explains the process. "Will it hurt?" I ask. Derrick's wife takes my hand and squeezes it. "We are going to give her some medication to keep her comfortable. It may be quick, and it may take a while. You guys are welcome to stay as long as you like," she says. The priest gives Nina her last rights, and we all bow our heads to pray.

The nurses start the process of turning off the machines and removing tubes and lines. I realize I am holding my breath. The nurse gives her another dose of morphine and lets us know that she will fall into a deep sleep. Tears are streaming down my face. Nina's breathing becomes slow and shallow. Her time is nearing. Peace settles around the room. I know she will not be in any more pain. She will be whole, wherever she goes. The heart monitor indicates her heart is slowing. We surround her bed and hold each other. A few minutes pass, and her heart monitor goes silent. The family leaves after arrangements are made. I stayed a few minutes longer. I hold Nina's hand. I say a silent prayer and promise to keep things going as long as I can. That I loved her and missed her already.

The funeral is beautiful. She was a well-loved lady. Most of the community is here. A lot of them are local artists. I sat with the family. This is an honor. I am more than blessed and thankful for her family accepting me. After the funeral, Nina's church serves the family lunch. My phone vibrates with a text. I don't recognize the number.

I am sorry to hear of Nina's passing.

L: Who is this?

J: Jake

L: Thanks.

I know he means well, but it sends hatred through my veins. He is the last person I want to hear from. Derrick walks over to me, "Can I talk to you for a minute Lottie?" We walked into the hall outside the fellowship hall. "Are you holding up ok?" He asks.

"About as good as I can be, she was like a grandmother to me."

"We will all miss her. Thank you for taking care of her and keeping The Gallery tended to."

"It was my pleasure."

"I know this is probably a weird time to have this conversation. But Marie and I have decided to keep the Gallery open as long as we can, and we want you to run it full time for us."

"Is that something your mother would want?"

"Of course, it is. That Gallery was her pride and joy. I did want to mention that we are going to sell her home. We will help you with another place to live."

"I understand and I appreciate that. I will do my best to keep The Gallery alive."

I hug Derrick and his family. I decided to go take a walk down at the park near the house. I think about Nina and how I hope her last days were filled with joy and love, despite having Alzheimer's. I miss her and love her so much. I have some big shoes to fill.

~ 9 ~

It's been a full year since Nina's death. The past year has been a difficult one. Amanda's husband took a new job in Texas. They moved a month after Nina's death. So, I've been alone. I keep to myself. Just home and The Gallery. I talk to Amanda, but no one else. Derrick checks in from time to time. I have fallen into a depression that I can't seem to shake. The Gallery isn't doing well at all. I am unable to keep workers, and the art we have is not selling. Not even Nina's work. Which is sad really. Her artwork is beautiful. After speaking to the Tenney family, the decision is made to shut down The Gallery. We have to sell everything including the building. I hope whoever moves in here has as much success as The Gallery did, even though it's failed now. It doesn't take long to sell the remaining paintings we have. Some of Nina's friends stop by. I take time to chat with each one. I hear stories about Nina I've never heard before. My heart swells.

I have been toying with the option of staying in Birmingham or moving back home. Honestly, I have nothing left here. My best friend has moved, and my other best friend is six feet under. The choice seems obvious since there is nothing left for me here. I made enough to keep my bills paid and also save. I call my momma. "Momma, can I come home?" I ask. "Honey, you never have to ask to come back home," she says. I hate everything about this, but I need my parents more now than ever. Thomasville may be the hell I ran away from, but it's the same place that is going to be my blessing. I pack what few things I want to take with me and sell everything else. For the first time in ten years, I'm headed home.

~ 10 ~

Mr. Curly is a mean old rooster that belongs to Samantha. It's five in the morning, and he decides it's time to start crowing. I woke up with a jolt and looked at the clock. I groan and lay back down, covering my head with the pillow. After about an hour of listening to that damn rooster, I got up. I take a shower and get dressed.

"Momma, I thought we were going to kill that bird and eat him for dinner," I say, coming down the stairs into the kitchen. "Lottie Mae, you know we can't do that, it would shatter your sister to pieces. Want some coffee?" she asks as she pours herself a cup, "And the problem with that is? I say. Momma rolls her eyes, "You better go out to the coop and get some eggs for breakfast before your father comes down." The eggs our chickens produce are the best in the county. Momma sells them to the local café and the small Farmers Market.

Daddy is sitting in his usual spot at the table reading the paper. He usually is up before Mr. Curly's ungodly crowing. "Sugar, you look tired," he says, stirring his coffee. "Yeah well, you can think that wretched rooster for that," I responded. Daddy has a smile on his face, "Oh no, don't be upset with that rooster. He is old and dead set in his ways. Best alarm clock around." I snort. "You know if he mysteriously disappears, you can just tell Samantha something ate him."

After breakfast, I help Daddy feed the horses. I lay on the couch and watch tv till the library opens. Momma and Daddy don't own a computer or have the internet (They are old school.) I plan on filling applications out for some places in Huntsville and Chattanooga. I miss working around art. "You want a ride to town? I can drop you off and pick you up after I get my errands done," Momma asks me. "You know you don't have to drive me everywhere, I have my car," I say. Daddy kisses Momma, "Now you let your momma drive you to town, she is excited to have you home." I agree and wash up.

Thomasville still looks the same except for a few new stores and a diner. I stare out the window as Momma drones on about what's been happening in the town. Who married who, who had kids, who got caught streaking through town. I manage a chuckle. "Well, here is your stop. I will be back at about 10," she reaches over and plants a kiss on my forehead. I have a flashback of my childhood. This was one of my favorite places. When I walk in, the place hasn't changed much.

"Lottie May Haywood, as I live and breathe," The woman at the counter yells across the room. "I'm sorry?" I ask. I have no idea who this person is. "Girl it's me, Natalie Spears, remember?"

"Oh, Hey. I didn't recognize you." Yeah, still no clue.

"We used to run wild together when we were younger." Then it dawns on me who she is. She had a nose job. I stifle a giggle. We stand and talk for a good fifteen minutes. She tells me all about her life since school. I look at my watch, "Well friend I need to get some stuff done online before my mother comes back." Natalie goes over the rules for the computers. They haven't changed in years. I just go with the flow. I nod and agree and take a seat at one near the back of the area. I set to work and apply at galleries in Huntsville and Chattanooga. I need a job while I'm here, so I looked up the number for the bar out on 411.

Momma pulls up exactly at ten o'clock. She chats on and on. "Memorial Day is next week, and we need to start planning the BBQ. We'll get a list at church Wednesday night. Your Daddy is going to pick a few cattle to take to the Butcher on Tuesday." This makes my stomach heave. I know it's the way of life, but I could have done without that detail. "How morbid," I say. "Now Lottie, don't start any of that crap. Daddy wants you to make the banana pudding. He doesn't like anyone else's," she says.

When we get home, I help Momma most of the day. I follow her around with a little notebook and make a list of everything she needs to do and get from the store. We have a big BBQ every year. Daddy says the whole town is coming this year. He says everyone is happy to have me home and they all want to see me. This is kind of funny to me, because I stayed in trouble, and I'm pretty sure half the town doesn't care for me. The thought makes me smile.

I decided to get a job at the local bar. I could work at the café or diner, but the bar sounds more fun to me. The bar doesn't open 'til four. I decided to take a nap. Momma knocks at the door, "Child, are you going to sleep the day away? It's time for supper." I raise up and look at the clock. I slept 'til 6. I jump out of bed and change clothes then head downstairs.

The Broken Wagon Saloon is a honky-tonk that has been around for as long as I can remember. Duke Riley has been its owner for the past twenty years. His great grandfather opened it up in 1952 and ran it till his passing. It was passed down from father to son. When I was a teenager, my friends and I would come here to two-step, and, depending on the bartender, we would drink one or two beers. Not much has changed about the place aside from a few upgrades. After four generations it's still the dusty old honky-tonk it has always been. People seem to like it that way.

The place isn't busy yet, and I am thankful I don't see anyone I know. I want to make this as short and sweet as possible. I want to get back home and relax. I've been so exhausted the last few months, exhaustion is hitting me all at once. "Excuse me, is Duke in?" I ask, walking up to the bar. The bartender turns around. He is tall and handsome, and I can say his ass looks good in those jeans. "Evan Riley?" I ask, shock across my face. "Lottie Mae Haywood. Damn you filled out," he says with a smile on his face. I feel my face turn red, "You grew into your ears," I say, letting out a chuckle. Evan wiggles his ears.

While we wait for Duke to come out of the office, Evan and I chit-chat and catch up. When we were kids, Evan was in love with me. He was my shadow. He was tall and lanky. His ears were too big for his head. He sure did grow up though. "Well, if it ain't trouble that has walked through my door.

Better call the five-o," Duke says, grabbing me in a bear hug. I guess he got over me stealing his pigs when I was a kid, I was trying my best to save them from the slaughter. The Rileys and the Haywoods have been good friends for years. They live on the farm next to us. I follow Duke into the office. "It won't be a problem for you to work here. You are welcome as long as you need to. I know your momma and daddy are happy to have you home," he takes a swig of his whiskey. Mr. Riley will talk your ear off if you let him. I try to wrap up the conversion up so I can get back home.

We say our goodbyes, and I stop back by the bar to say goodbye to Evan. He goes over the basics. I'm not worried about the waitressing part, that I have down pat. I've never been a bartender before, but I am a fast learner. "See you Thursday," Evan says, "It was really good to see you." I gave him a wave," I'll be here." The Broken Wagon is closed on Sundays and Wednesdays. Duke says it's so everyone can go to church. Patrons tend to just go to other bars on those days. I don't mind it though. At least it's consistent. I never had that at Walter's. Daddy is asleep in his chair when I get home. I cover him with a blanket. I guess he was going to wait for me, bless him. I kiss his cheek and head upstairs. I fall asleep as soon as my head hits the pillow.

I don't want to go to church, but Momma wants me to go. Tonight, is the fellowship dinner. Our church does this twice a month. There is no bible study. Momma works the room, chatting and dishing on gossip. I follow her around, shake hands, and hug the ones that hug me. I stay quiet. While Momma is talking to Mrs. Moore about next week, I spot Evan across the room. He sees me and flashes a smile in my direction. I return the smile and awkwardly give him a thumbs up. Mrs. Moore starts talking to me, but I'm barely listening. I can't keep my eyes off Evan.

I feel like I have been standing here forever while Momma makes her rounds. Finally, we fix our plates and sit down. I don't waste any time digging in. I'm starving. I haven't had my Momma's chicken and dressing in years. She only makes it for the Fellowship Dinner. Just as I'm shoving the last of my dressing in my mouth, the Rileys come over and sit with us. I became very aware of Evan sitting across from me. We make small talk, and I can't seem to stop smiling. Momma looks over at me and nods in approval. I haven't been in this good of a mood in a while.

Evan gets up and goes to get some dessert. He gets my attention and nods towards the door. I excuse myself and follow him outside. "Here, I got you some Mrs. Moore's Pecan Pie. It's the best around," He says handing me a plate, "I thought you needed to get some air." I take the plate from his hand and my fingers brush his. I blush and take a bite of pie. It is the best pie I've ever had. Mrs. Moore might be crazy, but she can bake a pie like no one's business. Evan smiles.

We talk between bites. Evan is easy to talk to. I try to relax and enjoy the moment. "You know, I'm glad you're back," he says. "I'd never thought I would be back. But it's just temporary I hope." I say as I hop up on the tailgate of his truck. We talk a lot about nothing. Daddy opens the door, "We are leaving. Your Momma is finishing up." I nod. "Well, I guess I better help Momma," I say. We both smile at each other and look away. "I was wondering," Evan says, helping me down off the tailgate, "You want to have a beer after your shift tomorrow?" I give it a few minutes. "I'd like that. We can catch up more," I say. He leans over and kisses my cheek (great, that heart skipping thing is back).

I stayed quiet on the way home. Momma and Daddy are talking about the BBQ. I think about everything that has happened. Where I am now versus where I was a few weeks ago. I shoot a text to Amanda.

L: I miss you. Tell Nate I love him.

A: We miss you! We will talk soon!

I miss Nina so much. I wish I could talk to her. I miss her wisdom and outlook on life. "Better get some sleep tonight. You have a big day tomorrow. I'm going to need help in the morning. Don't worry though, you will have enough time to nap before you start work," Daddy says as we get out of the car. I would much rather sleep in, but it will be nice to get back in the saddle again. I'm looking forward to spending time with Daddy.

~ 11 ~

We are done with all the work by the time lunch rolls around. Momma made some sandwiches and a homemade strawberry cake. At this rate, I'm going to balloon up. "Samantha called while you guys were out. She is coming home for the BBQ. She is bringing someone," Momma says as she sits down at the table. I roll my eyes. I haven't seen Samantha in years. We aren't close and that is fine by me.

It's not that I don't like her. She is my sister. We are just complete opposites. We fought a lot as kids, and I am pretty sure we are solely responsible for every gray hair on Daddy's head. I concentrate on my sandwich while Momma and Daddy talk about Samantha and her apparent new beau. I finish eating and head upstairs to try and sleep some. It's been a while since I worked at night, so I have to get into the groove. I'm not looking forward to seeing Samantha, but part of me wants to mend fences. I've learned that family is important. So, I'm going to try and make the most of it.

I decided to dress kind of sexy tonight. I go with a black tank top and blue jeans. I found my old pair of boots in my closet, and to my surprise, they still fit. I check myself in the mirror. I look pretty hot. Hopefully, I will make a lot of tips tonight. I yell at Momma and Daddy that I am leaving and try to sneak out before Daddy sees me. Momma sees me though and winks at me. She approved, but my Daddy would have a duck fit.

The bartending seems pretty simple. There aren't any special requests or fancy drinks. Just beer and whiskey. It starts getting busy around 7. My feet are hurting, but I am handling it like a pro. Evan has been working alongside me. He does most of the heavy lifting, so I don't have to. We make a pretty good team. After my shift, Evan brings a pitcher of beer and we sit in the back booth. I nurse my beer and try to relax. The conversation is light for the most part. He tells me about what he has been up to since we graduated high school. I tell him about my life too. I leave out the part about Jake. That's a conversation for another time. He takes me for a spin around the dance floor, and man can he move. His arms are strong, and I love the way his arms feel around my waist.

I make it home around midnight. I take my boots off when I get out of the car. My feet are throbbing. I promise myself to wear tennis shoes to work from now on. As I lay down, my phone goes off. It's a text from Evan:

E: You were wonderful tonight. You did such a good job.

L: Thank you. It was a good night.

E: Think I can take you out this weekend?

L: Sure. See you tomorrow.

"I have a date this weekend," I announced to the table. "Oh, is it with Evan?" Momma asks, topping off my coffee. "It is. Duke is closing the bar this weekend, so we are going to hang out," I reply. Daddy is halfway through his toast, "That Riley boy? He is the dumbest smartest person I know. Is he still going after you after all these years?" Momma lets out a laugh. "Leave her alone Sammy, let her have her fun," Momma says, squeezing my hand.

We finish breakfast and I set out to get a few errands done. I haven't heard from any of the places I applied for. It's ok. Sometimes these things take time. The first thing I do is buy some more clothes for work. I try to get some color into my wardrobe. I got some painting supplies and a notebook. I want to get back to painting again. I haven't done it in so long. It's time to get back to me. The next two days have been super busy at work and the farm. I help mom get a lot done for the BBQ. Evan tells me to be ready early Saturday morning. I can't wait.

Evan picks me up around seven in the morning. We head out to Trade Day. I haven't been in years. We walk around, eating corn dogs, and drinking lemonade. I bought some produce and a few plants for Momma. We head back to the farm. Daddy and some friends and a couple of the football players from the school are working on setting up the tables and chairs for the BBQ. Momma and Daddy have gone all out. There is even a bouncy house for the kids. "I can't wait to give that thing a whirl," I say. Even chuckles. "You want to go horseback riding?" He asked me. I agree and we walk hand in hand to the barn. We get the horses saddled up and head out into the pasture. He leads out into the back pasture where the pond is.

When we reach the shade tree, there is a basket full of sandwiches and beer. "I figured we could have a little lunch out here. It's pretty and all but not compared to you," Evan says, helping me off my horse. He is just so sweet. "You are too cute, thank you for this," I say. We sit and talk and eat and drink. Evan pulls me into his lap. It's nice to be held like this. I haven't felt butterflies like this since Jake, but I try to enjoy the moment. I'm not looking for a relationship. I don't want one. It's nice to spend time with Evan though. It brings back memories.

We finished our lunch. I start to clean up when Evan takes my hand, "Leave it. I'll come back out in a bit and grab it" Evan pulls me into him. I can feel the electricity pulsing through us. He lifts my chin and kisses me softly. I return the kiss, and it turns a little intense. There is urgency in his kiss, but I back away. "I'm not ready," I say. He nods and kisses me again, "It's ok, beautiful. You are worth waiting for." He got me there. I melt. We head back toward the house. I have to help Momma get some stuff done.

When we reach the barn, I see Samantha's car in the driveway. I wish I had taken a Xanax this morning. It's hard to deal with her without some kind of intervention. I remind myself that I want to try and mend the fences. I cringe when I hear her yell across the yard, "LOTTIE MAE HAYWOOD, YOU GET OVER HERE AND LET ME HUG YOUR NECK!" I turn to

Evan. He is giggling. I roll my eyes and give him a quick kiss. "I'll text you. Be safe," I say. "Always. See you tomorrow." When he drives off, I head toward the house. "Was that Evan Riley?" I nod, then hug her. "He grew into his ears," she says. I laugh. So far so good.

Momma is in the kitchen with Daddy. Momma is zipping around the kitchen and Daddy is supervising like always. I start pulling out the stuff to make the banana pudding. I want it to sit overnight so it will be good for tomorrow. Everyone is chatting about this and that. It feels good to be a family. "I have something to tell you guys," Samantha says, we all turn to look at her. "I'm engaged!" She exclaims. Daddy's eyes bug out of his face as he chokes on his sweet tea. Momma drops the spoon she is using to mix the coleslaw on the floor. I turn around and blankly stare at her. "Well, that's wonderful but who is he? We didn't know you were seeing anyone," Momma asks.

"Oh, he is nice. Handsome, too. And he has money. I'm marrying up y'all. You will get to meet him tomorrow. He is driving up in the morning," she says. Daddy leaves the kitchen when Momma and Samantha start talking about wedding stuff. God love him. "I want to have the wedding here at the farm, Momma," Samantha says.

"We can do that, when is the wedding?" Momma asks.

"Three months from now."

"Wait. What?" I ask, "Why so fast? How long have you guys been together?"

"Why does it matter? When you know, you know, right?"

"I guess we should get to planning then," Momma says as she finishes with the coleslaw.

Samantha, always with the dramatics. "I want you to be my Maid of Honor," Samantha walks up behind me and hugs me. My eye twitches. I agree and tell her not to put me in a God-awful dress. I finish with the pudding and take it out to the big fridge in the garage. I think about Evan.

E: What's the most gorgeous girl doing right now?

L: Just cleaning up. Was thinking about you.

E: Think I can steal you away?

L: I'll meet you out at the barn.

~ 12 ~

Evan is waiting at the barn door. I guess he walked over here, so he wouldn't wake my parents up. I feel like a teenager again. "Don't wake my parents up. You'll get me grounded," I said nodding towards the house. Evan laughs and pulls me through the door. He holds me in an embrace and starts to slow dance. "There is no music," I say. Evan smiles, "We don't need any, just the beating of our hearts." Damn, he is good.

He pulls away and looks at me, "You are so beautiful Lottie." Heat is rising in my face. He cups my face with his hands and kisses me slowly and hard. I give in. I can't help myself. He takes a blanket from the tack room, and we head up to the loft. We are kissing and shedding our clothes at a quick pace. Evan can't keep his hands off me. He kisses every inch of my body. We make love. Afterward, we are tangled up in each other. Evan wraps the blanket snugly around me. We talked for a while. I tell him about Jake. "I would never hurt you," Evan says. "Can we just take things slow? See where it leads?" I ask, my hands shake. "I'm willing if you are," he says. We fall asleep holding each other.

I wake with a start. I don't know what time it is, but the sun is up. "Evan, wake up!" I say nudging him awake. "Shit. We slept here all night," He laughs. We quickly get dressed and sneak out of the barn. No one is around. Evan kisses me quickly and heads back to his house. I plan on getting upstairs using the stairs in the kitchen. As soon as I walk in the door, Momma, Daddy, and Samantha are sitting at the table. They are staring at me. "Good morning everyone," I say. "Girl, where have you been?" Daddy says sipping his coffee. Momma has a grin on her face, and Samantha points at the hay in my hair. I quickly pick the pieces out of my hair before Daddy notices. "Um... out," I say awkwardly. "Looks like she had a roll in the hay," Samantha says with a chuckle. I blush. I could kick her.

I head upstairs to shower and change. I check my phone:

E: Did you get grounded?

L: LOL No.

E: See you for the BBQ. Miss you.

L: Miss you.

The tables are set up and people are starting to show up. I help Momma finish putting out the food. Everyone is having a good time. There is cornhole and horseshoes. The kids are loving the bouncy house. Momma was right when she said the whole town was coming. Samantha is working the crowd. She is eating up all the attention. I shake my head and turn back to my plate.

Evan and I are playing cornhole against Momma and Daddy when a Lincoln Navigator pulls in the drive. Samantha heads over to the vehicle. She disappears on the other side. "That must be Samantha's boyfriend," I say, nudging Evan. We all are watching the vehicle. After a few minutes, Samantha comes back around with a man. He is wearing a t-shirt, jeans, and a baseball cap. I can't see what he looks like from here. Momma and Daddy start walking towards Samantha, I take Evan's hand and we follow them.

The closer we get, the better I can see his features. I feel the color drain from my face. I have a pit in my stomach. I cannot believe what I am seeing. I start to feel a little nauseous and lean on Evan. "Baby, you ok?" he asks. "Yeah. A little hot," I lied. We finally meet in the middle. "Momma, Daddy, Lottie, I want you to meet Jake Samford," Samantha says, "And this is Evan Riley, Lottie's love interest." Now I want to punch her. Jake and I stare at each other with shock on our faces. Momma and Daddy both shoot me a glance. They are shocked too. Jake shakes hands with Daddy and hugs Momma. Jake goes in for a hug, and I stiffen. It's so awkward. I kind of hugged him back. "It's nice to meet all of you," he says.

Did he know? He can't. He was just as surprised as I was. Samantha has a habit of not telling anyone about her family or where she is from. I'm not sure why she does that. There had to be a point in the relationship where he was wondering where she was from and where she grew up. Did he not put two and two together? I feel like I'm going to throw up. "I need some water," I say. I squeeze Evan's hand to tell him I'm ok. I rushed back to the house.

I gulp down a glass of water and splash my face. I stand bracing myself at the sink. I have a million thoughts and questions going through my head. I hear the door open, and Jake walks in. "What the fuck are you doing here, is this a joke?" I ask. "No. It's not," he says.

"You didn't know where you were going? Like the town, the name didn't ring a bell?"

"I didn't think anything of it honestly. Samantha doesn't talk much about where she is from. All I knew was that she told me she was from North Alabama. That's it, and I didn't ask."

"Oh, so everything I ever told you, you just forgot it? And you told me you never wanted to settle down?"

"Lottie, please."

"Go to hell," I say and go back outside. I stay as close to Evan as I possibly can. He knows something is wrong but doesn't ask. He just tries to soothe me. "Are you sure you're ok?" he asks. "Yeah, I'll tell you later, "I say. For now, I decide to not say anything to Samantha. I know Jake won't say anything either.

~ 13 ~

By the time the sun starts to set, most of the food is gone and most of the crowd has left. "Come on baby, let's walk," Evan says and takes my hand. Momma nods with approval. We start walking towards the barn. "You seemed a little tense back there," Evan says. We walked behind the barn. I lean up against the wall, suddenly so tired. "I was," I say. I take a deep breath, "That is Jake Samford. My ex-boyfriend."

"They guy you told me about?"

"The one and only."

"He and Samantha are getting married?"

"So."

"You don't have to worry about that anymore, ok? I'm going to take care of you."

"You are so precious, Evan Riley," I said, touching his cheek. He kisses my palm, then kisses me.

We walk back towards the house, and Evan helps Daddy with the tables. I go to the kitchen and help Momma clean up. It has been a great day overall. Evan is such an amazing person. I honestly have some feelings for him. But judging by the past, even though I know I shouldn't, I still want to take things slow with him. I don't want to jump in when there is a possibility that we aren't on the same page. I know that Evan might have some feelings, but I am not sure. I don't want to ask him either. I will let the chips fall where they may.

Samantha is out on the front porch with Momma. Jake has gone with Daddy to take the tables back to the church. I want to see what kind of information I can get out of Samantha about her relationship with Jake. Momma has told me before about what's been going on with Samantha and her life. I have never really talked to her. We just aren't close. I bring some sweet tea out for us and sit next to Momma on the porch swing.

"So, tell us about your beau, Samantha," Momma says. I sit back eager to hear what she has to say about Jake. "He is amazing. He works with his family's company. He is a partner. He is so sweet and caring. We have a lot of fun together. We met at a function for his mother's charity," she says. Momma and I look at each other. "That's nice dear. How long have you guys been together?" Momma asks. Samantha grins, "Six months." I choke on my tea. Momma pats me on the back. "That's not very long, Samantha, you barely know him," she says.

"Why so quick?" I ask. Samantha sits back and thinks for a moment. "Well, I know enough to know that he loves me. I mean, he wouldn't have asked me if he didn't," she says. I roll my eyes. My sister. So naïve. I know Jake and it makes me wonder. I know that one person may not be right for you, and they may be right for someone else. I can't wrap my head around it. It shouldn't matter, but for some reason, it's all I can think about. Samantha is droning on and on about Jake and the wedding. She wants to find a house here in Thomasville so that she can come to stay here sometimes. A summer home if you will. I shake my head.

My mind wanders to Evan. Reconnecting to him has been amazing. Handsome, kind, courteous, caring. That's Evan. He understands me and why I am hesitant. He is patient with me. I hate knowing that I may be leaving, and there is a possibility that our relationship may end. It is what it is.

~ 14 ~

The week has been busy. I still haven't heard from any of the galleries I applied to. I plan on going over to Evan's to use his internet. I'm slow to get out of bed and get ready. I'm excited to see Evan, but I dread going downstairs. I finally talked myself into getting out of bed. When I reach the kitchen, I peer around the door, checking to see if Jake is in the kitchen. So far, so far so good. I grab a muffin and head out the door.

As soon as I rounded the corner and headed to my car, I saw Jake on the phone out by his car. I look over at the chicken coop and then back to Jake. I get an idea, and I chuckle to myself. I sneak over to the coop, making sure Jake doesn't see me. I'm almost beside myself at what I'm about to do. "Ok Mr. Curly, we're about to have a little fun," I say. I pick him up and carry him over to the house. I hid around the corner. When I set the rooster down, he took off after Jake. I'm laughing so hard my stomach hurts. Mr. Curly is chasing him around the car. Jake runs towards the house and runs inside, looking out the door. I walk by and wave, still laughing.

I'm still smiling when I reach Evan's house. Evan is standing on the porch with his father. "What are you smiling for?" Duke asks, hugging me. I tell them both what I did. "You still got that mean streak, don't you?" he says. Evan chuckles and pulls me into a hug. Duke heads off to the bar, and Evan and I head into the house. Evan has a few things to tend to, so he leaves me alone to get my stuff done. After a while, he brings me a cup of coffee. "Still no luck?" he asks, kissing my forehead. "Not at all. I applied to more places. I hope I hear something soon," I replied. Evan and I spend the rest of the afternoon together before work. We do a whole lot of nothing.

The bar is slow for now, but I know it will get busy around eight o'clock. I take advantage and do some stocking, so I won't have to do it when people start pouring in. Suddenly I hear the doors fly open. It's Samantha, and she looks madder than a wet hen. She marches up to the bar, "What's this I hear about Mr. Curly chasing Jake all around the farm?" I snort. "I have no idea what you are talking about," I say with a shrug. "Then I guess it wasn't you that greased Jake's door handles either, was it?" She asks. I know she is mad because her eye is twitching. I can't help but giggle. "Lottie Mae Haywood, you stop your shit right now," she yells. "Oh Samantha, it was all in good fun. I was just welcoming him to the family," I say innocently. She rolls her eyes and storms out of the bar. Evan looks at me with raised eyebrows. I shrug and get back to work.

The bar has gotten slower than usual, so Evan tells me I can head home. I kiss him goodbye and wave to Duke. When I reach the house, I shoot Evan a text letting him know I made it home safely. Jake is sitting in the kitchen working on stuff for work. I don't say anything to him. "You are such an ass-hole," he says as I walk past him. "Takes one to know one," I say, sticking my tongue out at him. Jake rolls his eyes, "Why do you hate me so much?"

"Why are you a jerk? You are stringing my poor sister along."

"What? No, I'm not."

"You are. If I remember correctly, you never wanted to settle down. No family. You wanted to have your cake and eat it, too. Tell me something, are you still seeing Sarah?"

"Things change, Lottie. They do."

"What a bunch of bullshit"

"It's not bullshit. I do love your sister."

"Whatever."

I march upstairs and slam the door. Jake makes me so mad I could spit nails. I'm sure Samantha did something to make him want to settle down. I'm a little jealous. Why does he want her, and he doesn't want me? Is it because he and I were from different worlds? The joke is on him though because Samantha is from the same world I am. I'm just not the bubbly blonde my sister is.

I'm tired and grumpy by the time morning arrives. I didn't sleep well. When I come down to the kitchen, Daddy is sitting at the table eating breakfast and reading the paper. "I heard you were up to a little mischief yesterday," he says, sipping his coffee. I smirk, "I was, I had a good laugh." He laughs, "That's my girl," he says. I love my Daddy. We sit and talk over breakfast. Momma and Samantha have gone to Huntsville to shop for wedding things, and Jake has gone back to Birmingham for the rest of the week. Thank God.

I decided since I don't have to work today, I'm going to do some painting, and maybe some reading. I'm hoping to take it easy today. My anxiety has been on edge since the BBQ. It's a major cluster in my book. My phone chimes. I'm hoping it's Evan, but frown when it's not.

J: Whatcha doing?

L: Why does it matter to you?

J: I was just wondering.

L: I'm sure.

J: I'm just trying to be friendly here.

L: You and I are not friends.

J: Lottie.

L: Does Samantha know you are texting me?

That ended the conversation. Jake doesn't text back. I settle down and get to work. Painting is so soothing to me. Nina comes to my mind. I wonder what she would say about this situation. I miss her sage advice. I give Derrick a call and check on him and his family. They are doing well which makes my heart happy. They sort of have become family.

"Hey beautiful," Evan says walking up behind me. It makes me jump. "I'm going to put a bell on you," I say giggling. I kissed him. "That would defeat the element of surprise, wouldn't it," he says. I smile from ear to ear. We sit and talk while I work. "You want to have dinner with me tonight?" he asks. "Of course, I would," I say. When I get to a stopping point, I clean up. "I will be back at six," Evan says, kissing me. I take a long soaking bath and get ready for tonight. I want to look good. It's hot so I chose a little sundress and sandals.

Six o'clock rolled around so I headed downstairs. Evan is already here. He looks so hot. He has blue jeans with boots on and a checkered button-up shirt on. He is on the couch talking to my parents. "Honey, you look wonderful," Momma says. I smile. Evan picks up the bouquet he brought me, "These are for you." Momma nods in approval. "Thank you, they are lovely," I say. I kiss his cheek, and Momma takes them to put them into a vase. "Treat my girl right son," Daddy says. He shakes Evan's hand. "Always," Evan replies and takes my hand. This is our real first date with each other. I'm excited and nervous even though I've been spending time with him. We drove up to Ft. Payne for dinner. We laughed and talked and ate good food. It was wonderful. I haven't smiled this much in a while. It makes my heart happy.

The sun is setting and it's showing out. It's gorgeous. We walk hand in hand through the park. We steal kisses from each other. "Hey, the fair is in town, do you want to go?"

Evan asks. "Sounds fun," I replied. We finish out the night riding rides and eating funnel cakes. Evan wins me a stuffed cow. I giggle when he hands it to me. It's been a wonderful evening. I needed this. Evan is so simple. He doesn't try to impress me. It's comfortable being around him and I feel like I can tell him anything.

It's about eleven o'clock when we get back to the farm. I've had so much fun I don't want the night to end. We stand by the truck for a good while, kissing and holding each other. We finally unhinge from each other. We are both out of breath and smiling at each other. "Can I talk to you about something?' Evan asks. My heart skips a beat and the butterflies are back. "Sure," I say, biting my lip. He pushes my hair behind my ear and caresses my cheek. I know I'm blushing and I'm the color of a tomato. "You are so beautiful. I've enjoyed spending time with you since you have been back," He says and takes my hand, "You are such an amazing woman."

"I think you need your eyes checked."

"No baby. I don't."

"I've had fun with you. It's been great. I haven't been this happy in a while."

"I have feelings for you, Lottie."

"Is that right?"

"Yes."

"I don't know what to say," I replied. Evan stares at his boots. "I have feelings for you, too," I say after a few moments. He looks up at me and smiles that smile I love so much. I see Momma and Samantha peering through the window. I motion for them to go away. Evan doesn't notice. "You want to go steady?" He asked me. I snort, "What are we, in high school?" He giggles and says, "You know what I mean." "I'm your girl," I say, kissing him. "Good night Lottie Mae, I'll call you tomorrow," he says after he hugs me. We kissed goodnight.

Samantha and Momma are sitting in the living room making themselves busy as if they weren't spying on me. "Well, how did it go?" Momma asks. "Yeah, how did it go?" Samantha asks with a suggestive look. I laugh and tell them about the date. "He has feelings for me, I feel the same way," I say. Samantha whistles and Momma smiles with approval. "Y'all stop," I say smiling. "It's good to see you happy Lottie. It's been a long time coming," Momma says. Samantha follows me upstairs.

"Evan Riley, who would have thought out of all the people," Samantha says, laying down on the bed. "It's not like it's a shock. We played together as kids," I said. "So, tell me, what have you been up to since the last time we saw each other?" Samantha asks. I tell her about the gallery, Nina and Amanda. I tell her I was with someone, but I leave Jake's name out of it. We talked for a good while. Samantha tells me her plans for the wedding. It makes me want to gag, but I listen and fake smile in all the right places. She wants to go dress shopping tomorrow. I dread it.

We set out after breakfast to go to Huntsville to find Samantha's wedding dress. I get she is excited, but it is getting on my nerves. We make a huge loop from Huntsville, to Albertville, to Ft. Payne. Finally, after about eight stores, she finds the perfect one. It is a gorgeous white mermaid-style gown with crystals all over it. She looks stunning. Momma cried. I feel my phone vibrate. It's a text from Evan.

E: Thinking of you. See you at work tonight.

The night is super busy with it being the weekend. My feet are throbbing so bad. I tell Evan about the dress and what Samantha plans on having the bridesmaid's dresses look like. He smirks at me but tells me I could be in a potato sack, and I would still be beautiful to him. I steal a quick kiss before the next customer comes to the bar. Duke scowls at us and shakes a finger. I duck around Evan and get back to work.

~ 15 ~

Daddy is still up when I get home from work. "What are you doing up so late Daddy?" I ask him and kiss his forehead. "I couldn't sleep. So, I came downstairs to do a little reading," he says. He pats the seat next to him on the couch for me to sit next to him. "I hear you had a good date with that Evan boy," he says. I snort, "I did. We had a lot of fun," I say. "That's good. I know you haven't been in the best of moods lately," He replies. I lean my head on his shoulder, "I haven't with everything that has happened." Daddy stays silent for a moment and asks, "How do you feel about Samantha and Jake?"

"I think it's doomed for failure."

"Why is that?"

"Well based on what I have been told before, I don't think Jake is ready to settle down."

"Maybe he is. Things can change sugar."

"I know they do. It's frustrating though."

I let out a big sigh. "You have a good man in Evan. He adores you and me and your Momma likes him just fine. I'd rather see you happy than stressed out over someone that doesn't want a future," he says. "Then why is he settling down now?" I ask. Daddy shrugs his shoulders, "Sometimes, one person isn't right for you, but right for someone else. Don't go worrying about all that. Just be happy," he says. Daddy and I think a lot alike. "Do you like Jake?" I ask him.

"I like him ok. He seems like he is right up Samantha's alley. He ain't no country boy, I can tell you that," He says after a few minutes. I laugh and hug him. "We should head to bed," I say and head up the stairs. "I love you, Daddy," I say. "I love you too, sugar," he says and hugs me. I think about what Daddy said. I know he is right. I do have a good man in Evan, and I don't need to focus on Jake and his reasons.

I slept in. Sleep was restless. I tossed and turned. I call Evan and tell him I won't be in tonight for work. It was weird to call in. I never have before, but Evan knows I've been exhausted. He tells me that it is ok, and to get some rest and that he will stop by to check on me. I smile. I fully intend to be as lazy as possible today. It is nearly noon when I make it downstairs. When I make it to the living room, I find Jake staring at my painting. "You did this?" he asks. I roll my eyes, and sit on the couch, pulling a big blanket over me (Momma keeps it frigid in the house). "I did. I painted it the other day," I replied. He turns around and looks at me, "It's really good. How come you never painted when we lived together?" I look at him blankly, "When did I ever have the time? Between work, you, and Nina I never had much time to myself." I don't feel like talking to Jake. I have too many questions and honestly, I don't have to have that conversation. I ignore him hoping he will go away.

Just when I am about to tell him to kick rocks, Samantha and Momma come through the door. They have bags and bags of stuff. "What's all that?" I ask. "Wedding stuff. We've been shopping all day. We got a lot of stuff here. We are going to make the centerpieces and Daddy is going to build an archway. We got some flowers and garland to decorate that. Want to help?" Samantha says. I respectfully decline and head back upstairs. I read some and listen to music. I watch some shows on my phone. I end up falling asleep. My phone vibrates and wakes me up.

E: How are you feeling baby?

L: I was napping, but I'm feeling better.

E: I'll be there in a little while when it dies down. I got you something.

L: You really shouldn't have. See you soon.

I meet Evan outside on the front porch. It's a beautiful night. You can see all the stars it seems like. Evan kisses me and sits next to me on the swing. We sit in silence and just enjoy each other's company. After a few minutes, he goes and gets something from his truck. It's a tiny box. He is grinning ear to ear when he comes back to the porch. "It's not much but I thought of you when I saw it," he says, handing me the box. It's a necklace with a pendant in the shape of a painter's pallet. "It's beautiful. I love it. You really shouldn't have," I say as I kiss his cheek. Evan helps me put it on. It's so thoughtful. Momma comes to the door to tell me dinner is ready. She offers a plate to Evan, and he accepts. We all enjoyed a meal together. This feels right. "I need to get back to the bar," he says. I walk him out and we kiss and hold each other. Daddy is right, he is a good man.

~ 16 ~

We are working cows today. It takes a lot of work, but it's one of my favorite things to do. "Lottie, I need you to go to the feed store for me. They have the order I put in, Take Jake with you," Daddy says. I start to protest but decide against it. I'll need help. Maybe it won't be bad. I have to get used to the idea that he will be my brother-in-law.

The ride to the feed store is mostly in silence. "You know you can talk," Jake says. I sit quietly concentrating on driving. "Earth to Lottie," Jake smirks. "I find it hard to believe you are getting married. To my sister. I can't help but wonder how she tagged and bagged you in six months," I say, finally. Jake doesn't speak for a moment. "Things change," he says. Things do change. "Why did you do me the way you did? What made you change your mind?" I ask.

"You didn't do anything. Sarah was a mistake. We were fine the way we were."

"So, you went from wanting everything you had, to not wanting it to, settling down?

"Well."

"Deep subject."

"Mom and Dad want me to settle down."

Now that I think about it, his mom never really liked me. She only spoke to me when she had to. Jake being an only kid, was a Momma's boy. What Momma wants, Momma gets, I guess. I know what his mom wants. High society, the same level as them. Money and greatness. Unfortunately, I don't fit that mold. "You mean your Mom wants you to settle down," I say, "Your Dad could care less."

"Lottie," he says. He tends to do that when he gets frustrated with me. He should be. I want answers. He changes the subject. He asks questions about finding work and what my life was like after we broke up. I told him. He tells me what he has been up to, but I don't pay attention. After we pick up the items at the feed store, the drive home is a little better. I find myself talking more. The ease with which we are carrying the conversation surprises me. "So, is that Evan guy your boyfriend?" Jake asks. "He is. Why?' I replied. After a moment, he turns and looks at me, "I was just wondering."

When we get back to the farm, Jake helps me unload everything. He follows me into the barn. He seems eager to learn the way of farm life, so I guess it's up to me to teach him. Daddy just gets frustrated when he tries to teach. It mostly ends up with everyone grumpy. "So, what does this whole 'working cows' thing entail?" Jake says. He is such a city boy. "We are going to separate cows, then tag the calves. We will vaccinate them and castrate some of them. Some of them are going to the sale. One or two are going to go to the butcher," I say. "I'm sorry, what?" he says. It looks like the color has drained from his face. I laugh.

Some of Daddy's friends have come to help. I saddle up the horses for me and Jake. He is a little apprehensive but gets on the horse anyways. We take it slow until he feels more comfortable. Samantha would kill me if he ended up hurt. We head out into the pasture and start rounding the cows up and lead them toward the barn. Once we get all the cows moved into the corral, we set to work. We kind of move in a production line. I show Jake how to tag the cows and give them the vaccines. We move the bulls into another corral. Jake seems a little green in the gills at this point.

Daddy gets to work on the bulls. I look over at Jake to tell him something, and he isn't standing next to me. I look down and he has passed out cold. I laugh and wake him up. When the work is done, I finish up and head back to the house. "You did well," I say to Jake. He is sitting on the porch with his head between his legs. I go in and get a wet wash-cloth and bring it out. "You could have warned me," he says as I place the cloth on his forehead. "I thought it was pretty self-explanatory," I replied. He scowls at me. I get us some tea and sit on the porch talking.

I guess Jake and I can be friends. Samantha pulls up after being gone all day and rushes to the porch. "Oh my god, baby! What happened?" she asks Jake. I roll my eyes and stand up. "He had his first dose of farm life. He will be fine," I say. I go into the house and get ready for work.

~ 17 ~

There is a month left before Samantha and Jake say 'I do'. Samantha is running around like a chicken with its head cut off. Jake is back and forth to Birmingham. Evan and I have been spending more time together. I must admit I kind of miss Jake. I hate to say it and I feel some guilt about it.

Samantha has an idea to have a joint bachelor and bachelorette party at the Broken Wagon. Duke agrees to open the bar on Wednesday for the party. Samantha has invited everyone. Jake's friends have come up from Birmingham. I plan on having fun tonight and letting loose. I haven't done that in ages. I called Amanda to check on her and her family. I fill her in on everything. She is excited for me. She hopes she can make it to visit soon. I miss her and Nate like crazy.

Everyone is dancing, drinking, and eating. We are all having a good time. Momma and Daddy left early to get home before dark. Evan and I are in the back booth watching everyone party. After a while, he leaves too. He and Duke are leaving in the morning for their annual fishing trip. One of Duke's friends is going to run the bar while he is gone, so I am glad I will be able to work. I join Samantha and Jake at the bar.

Samantha is three sheets to the wind. Daddy comes to pick her up. Jake stays behind. Jake asks me to dance, and I oblige.

I know I am tipsy, but it feels good in Jake's arms. It reminds me of old times. Jake is smiling at me when I look up at him. "What are you smiling about?" I ask. "I was just thinking about how we used to slow dance in the kitchen," he says after a moment. We talk about memories. I know Jake is tipsy too the way he is swaying.

Most of the crowd has died out. When the last person leaves, I start to lock up. I will come in tomorrow and clean the place up. I'm going to make Samantha help me since it was her party. While I'm at the bar gathering cups, Jake walks up behind me and puts his arms around my waist. "What are you doing?" I ask him. I feel him smile against my shoulder. He starts kissing my neck. "We shouldn't be doing this, Jake. You are getting married in less than a month. To my sister," I say. I don't do anything to stop him though. I turn around and kiss him, taking his hand and walking him towards the office. I lock the door as soon as we enter. We are all over each other and there is no sign of stopping.

I jolt awake. My head is pounding. I must have drunk too much last night. I remember bits and pieces of the night. The only ones I seem to remember are those with Jake. I jump up and get dressed and head out into the bar. The place is a mess. I check my phone and I have a few missed calls from Momma. I called her back and told her I stayed at the bar and slept in the office since I drank a lot. Once she is satisfied with my reasoning, I end the call. I have a text from Jake.

J: Going back to Birmingham for some business. I had a good night.

I ignore the message and head towards the door. As soon as I open the door, Evan is standing there with his hand stuck out. "Baby you look like hell," he says. I smile and kiss him. "I stayed here because I drank a lot last night. I didn't want to drive," I say, "I will be back in a little bit to clean this mess up." "Don't worry about it, I will have someone come and do it. You go home and get some rest," he says. I hope he didn't pick up on my weirdness. I tried to keep a straight face and act as nothing happened. I hurry to my car. I call Jake. "Did we, you know, do the things last night?" I ask. "Wow I thought you would remember something like that," he says. I don't have time for his shit today. "Listen to me, we don't tell anyone about this. Do you hear me? Not one breath," I say and hang up the call. My face is hot with tears.

I can't believe this has happened. I didn't stop him. I let him. He was drunk, too. This was just a drunken mistake. Samantha knocks on my door and I jump. "Hey, we are working on centerpieces, want to join us? I have wine" she asks. "Jesus, Samantha it is nine o'clock in the morning," I responded. "Hair of the dog," she smiles. I tell her I just want to sleep. My head is throbbing, and I am so hungover. Evan checks on me before he heads out. I hope he has a good time with his dad. I lay in bed and think about things that have happened over the past few days. I am mad at myself for letting this happened over the past few days. I am mad at myself for letting this happen. And it was with Jake. How stupid am I?

~ 18 ~

Work drags on and I don't have the energy to do anything. I'm still a little hungover, but not as bad as I was this morning. I chat with the patrons and serve beer. I plaster on a fake smile. I just want to get through the night. My mind is somewhere else tonight. I step into the office for a minute to have some time to myself. If things stayed the same, Jake and I would be married by now. Maybe even have a little one on the way. I think about Evan. I think about what the future holds for us. I can see us together for the rest of our lives and have a family. The feeling of guilt washes over me again. I finish out the night and head home,

When I get home, there are flowers on my dresser. They are pink and white Gerber daisies. They are gorgeous. I open the card and read it.

A BEAUTIFUL WOMAN SHOULD BE SURROUNDED BY BEAUTIFUL THINGS

It doesn't say who it's from, but I know who exactly sent them. I have another rush of guilt, but I smile. Part of me still has feelings for Jake. I don't think I ever really got over him. I filled my days after the breakup to keep my mind off of him and what happened. I lay awake a while and thought about the past. I finally fell asleep.

Samantha has all her wedding stuff spread out on the living room floor. It is mind-boggling to me the amount of planning that she is doing. Samantha is always the planner. Everything down to the last detail. It makes her good at her job. It makes my head hurt. "Do you need any help?" I asked her. She looks up at me with a crazed look in her eyes. "That would be nice. Momma has gone off to a meeting with the ladies of the church, I have no idea where Daddy is and Jake won't be back 'til the end of the week and I am losing my mind," she says. I sit down beside her and we work together. Honestly, it's nice. Maybe my sister and I can have a relationship.

"Thank you for your help. I think we got a lot done," she says. I smile and hug her. We clean up the mess and I get ready for work. I shoot Evan a text.

L: I miss you so much! I hope you're having fun.

E: I miss you baby. We are.

He sent me a few pictures of the trip. There is a lovely one of him and his dad with the big bass they caught. I think about getting it framed. My feelings for Evan are growing. I think I love him. I can't wait for him to get back. I miss him so much. I just want to be in his arms.

Samantha decided to have her bridal shower at the church for space-sake. All her friends are there. I don't know half of these people except the ladies of the church and the ones from town. I grit my teeth and push through the affair. I am not a big fan of social gatherings. Everyone is so bubbly and chatty. It's making me cringe. I at least attempted to dress for the part, in a floral sundress, as opposed to my black shirts and jeans or shorts. At least the food is good. Momma made her chicken and dressing again, and I am one hundred percent on board with that.

Samantha walks over to me and hugs me. I am happy for her. Sort of. "Are you having a good time? I know this isn't your forte?" She asks me. I fake smile, "Yeah, everything is so nice." What I wanted to say to her is that she is making a mistake. I keep my mouth shut though. I want her to learn on her own. Samantha does seem in love. Naive, but in love. Everything with Jake is just a mess. The feelings I have for Jake are coming back. I have no idea what to do. I have strong feelings for Evan. I love him. But what am I supposed to do?

My stomach is starting to hurt, and I feel nauseous. I get kind of clammy, so I sit down. Suddenly, I have the urge to throw up. I ran to the bathroom. After puking my guts up, I just sit there by the toilet with my head in my hands. I haven't had any wine, so I know it's not that. I haven't overeaten either. I mentally go through everything in my head. The more I think about it, the more it makes my head hurt. I realize I haven't had my period. How late am I? I do the calculations and figure out I am three weeks late. I've been so busy that I haven't noticed. Shit. I find Momma and Samantha and tell them I am not feeling well so I am going to go home.

I stop by the Dollar General and grab a couple of pregnancy tests. I lock myself in the bathroom, even though no one is home. I take two and save one in the morning. I wait a good five minutes just to be sure. They are both positive. Fuck me. The next morning, I took the last test. Positive. I feel sick to my stomach. I don't know what to do. The worst part is I have no idea who the father is. Jake or Evan. What a mess this is. For right now, I will not tell anyone. I made a phone call.

My appointment with the doctor isn't 'til one, and I am early. I am a nervous wreck. I can't seem to sit still. Finally, they called me back to a room. Dr. Williams looks the same now as he did when I was a kid. "Lottie Mae, look at you," he says as he enters the room. "Hi Dr. Williams," I replied. He gives me a bear hug. We catch up briefly and he asks what he can do for me. "Well, I believe I am pregnant," I say, a few tears escaping. He promises me he will take care of me. I have blood drawn. I pace the waiting room. Finally, Dr. Williams comes back in. "Well girl, looks like you have a bun in the oven. Congratulations," he says. My fears have just been confirmed. Tears well up in my eyes again. I don't know if I should be happy or sad. Either way, this is a cluster that's for sure. He gives me some medicine for nausea and sets up an appointment with an obstetrician. I thank him and head back home.

Evan is home from the fishing trip. I keep quiet about the pregnancy until I can figure out what to do. I stopped by his house on the way home. It's so good to see him after being gone for a week. I fill him in on what has been going on at the bar and what needs to be done. I told him about the bridal shower. "I've missed you so much," I say. "Baby I missed you," he replies, kissing my forehead. I listen to him tell me about the fishing trip, but I'm not listening. I'm dazed and in another world.

The wedding is less than two weeks away. I help Samantha and Momma as much as I can. Jake is back too. I try my hardest to avoid him, but he is around every corner. Momma and Samantha have gone to pick up her wedding dress and the bridesmaid dresses. Daddy is off piddling around. So, it's just me and Jake at the house. I'm curled up in Daddy's chair when Jake brings me a cup of tea. We make small talk, but mostly we stay silent. "Why don't you come over here," Jake says. I get up and he pulls me into his lap. "There, that's nice," he says as he pulls the blanket over us. I must admit it does feel nice laying here in his lap. "What are you thinking about?' I ask him.

"Why did I ever leave you?"

"I'm pretty sure I left you."

"That you did. I was shitty to you."

"It happens."

"I think about what could have been all the time."

"Even though you are marrying Samantha in two weeks?"

"Yea. I know it's wrong, but you are the one that got away."

"Are you having doubts?'

"Honestly?"

"Honestly."

"I am."

"Why?"

"Because I'm still in love with you."

This takes me by surprise. I am at a loss for words. I smile though. He knows I'm with Evan. I know I'm with Evan. At this moment though, I just let my mind wander. What exactly is Jake wanting here? Is he wanting me back? Is he realizing that he did want a future with me? I want to ask him these questions. I want to tell him about the pregnancy, even though I'm not sure yet if he is the father. This is a sticky situation.

We sat there for a while just snuggling and kissing. I hear a car door and jump up and look out the window. Momma and Samantha are back. Jake and I scramble to make it look like we weren't doing anything. Momma shakes her head when she walks into the kitchen. "I swear your sister is stubborn as a mule," she says. I nod without saying anything. Samantha walks in carrying my dress. "Time to try it on to see if it needs any alterations," she says. I follow her upstairs.

I slip on the dress, but I can't get it zipped. It's snug. Samantha tries and fails. "Lottie, what have you been eating? It seems like you've gained weight. We're going to have to let this dress out a little." I bite my lip and look up to the heavens." I don't know. It fit perfectly at the dress shop." She takes her measuring tape and measures my waist and shakes her head, "Good thing we have time. Better go on a diet." I fight the urge to stick my tongue out at her.

"Come on in here, I want to talk to you," Momma says. I sit down at the table and Momma places a cup of tea in front of me. "Is there anything you want to tell me?" she asks. I stiffen up and look everywhere but her. I think she knows. I tread lightly, "What do you mean?" She looks at me with a squint. "Well, judging by the number of pickles in the fridge, and you puking at any given moment, I figure something is up," she says. Yeah, she knows. She just wants to hear me say it.

"I have something to tell you, but you can't say anything. Not just yet," I say, looking down at my cup, "I'm pregnant." Her face lights up and she is smiling from ear to ear. I think for a moment and take a deep breath, "I don't know who the father is." Momma doesn't say anything for a good five minutes. "Who do you think it is?" she asks. This conversation is hard, especially with my Momma. I think it would be worse with Daddy. "It's either Evan's," I say. "Or?" Momma says, waiting for me to stop beating around the bush. "or Jake's."

Momma sits there. She doesn't say anything. I am trying to judge her reaction. Either she is in shock, or she is not surprised. I brace myself. "This is quite the pickle you are in," she finally says. This is the kind of trouble Samantha would get herself into. Not me. I'm the good one. "Well, we will figure it out," she says, hugging me. I ask her to keep it between us only until I can figure out what to do. She is right, this is quite the pickle. Daddy comes in and I tell him the news. I leave out what Momma and I talked about. He is so excited to have a grandchild. I ask him not to tell anyone just yet. He kisses my forehead and hugs me.

I talk with Duke and Evan and decide to take a few days off for personal reasons. Also, because Samantha's wedding is Saturday, and she needs a lot of help. The planning for the wedding has been crazy. It makes my head hurt. I helped as much as I could.

~ 19 ~

"That's your second jar of pickles," Evan says as he walks into my room. "Ok, and?" I ask sarcastically. I try to make it look perfectly normal. I hope he doesn't pick up on it. He shakes his head and smiles, leaning down to kiss me. "It's time to go," he says. I slip my shoes on and take his hand. Samantha had decided to have the wedding at the church as opposed to having it at the house outside. She doesn't want to have to deal with the weather. We are headed there to help decorate.

Daddy and Jake are putting together the archway and Evan and I are on balloon detail. "Could this wedding get any gaudier?" I ask. Evan just laughs and says, "My mom always said the gaudier the better." We giggle. How could I ever throw away what Evan and I have, over one drunken mistake? I hope this is Evan's baby. A small part of me hope's it's Jake.

Jake steals glances at me and Evan. He looks annoyed. I know he is jealous. I don't envy him though. He is the one that has to put up with my sister for the rest of his life. That is a feat in itself. Evan would be a wonderful father. Jake would be too. I get a wave of nausea. "You ok baby?" Evan asks. "I'm

98

fine. I need to go to the restroom," I say. I rush to the bathroom hoping I don't throw up. I take a pill and wait for nausea to subside. I splash my face with water.

When I get back to the sanctuary, Evan looks worried. I tell him it's a stomach bug, but I'm fine. Jake looks at me and I nod my head. I watch Samantha as she walks around and supervises. I think she is way over her head. Jake is not the man she thinks he is. Not because of the way he was when we were together, but because of the way he has been with me since she introduced him.

Most of everyone has gone home, leaving me and Samantha finishing up everything. "Honey, you don't look so well," she says, pulling a chair up for me to sit down. "I'm fine," I say. She offers me a glass of wine, but I decline. "That's new. What's with that jar of pickles? You've been eating them like crazy. It's almost like you are pregnant," she says. Great. "OH MY GOD!" she shrieks. "Keep your voice down. No one knows," I say. She asks so many questions, "Evan is going to be such a good daddy. Let's hope the kid doesn't have his big ears," she says. I do laugh at that. "Please, for all holy things, don't say anything, ok? No one knows but Momma," I say. This is going to be the ultimate test. Samantha doesn't know how to keep her mouth shut at all. "It explains the letting out of the dress," she laughs. I want to punch her.

We head home, and Samantha hasn't stopped talking since we left the church. "Are you sure you want to marry Jake?" I ask.

"Absolutely. He is a wonderful man. Good looking. He has money. Great family. What more could I want?"

I roll my eyes. "It's all so fast though."

"Love knows no time."

"Yes, but have you thought about it, really thought about it?"

"Yes, I have. This is what I want."

"Is it though? These types of decisions shouldn't be made on a whim."

"You are just jealous."

"I am not."

"You are. You are jealous of my happiness. The guy you were with before Evan didn't want you and now here you are pregnant and not married. Despite everything you have been miserable since you came home. And I'm happy and you can't stand it."

"You are such a bitch. You have no idea what I've been going through. You didn't even bother to call. And I know Momma has told you a lot. You are making a mistake. Just go ahead and ruin your life."

"As far as I'm concerned, my life isn't the one that is ruined."

"Fuck you."

"You're out of the wedding."

I slam the door of the car and march upstairs to my room. She infuriates me to no end. I can't believe she is still a bitch after all these years. I guess being a good sister is out the window now.

J: Hey what happened with you and Samantha?

L: We fought. It's fine.

J: Where are you?

L: I'm about to go to Evan's

J: She said I should ask you what's been going on.

L: It's not your business.

I head to Evan's. I'm so upset, and he is the only person I want to see right now. Not Momma and Daddy. Not Jake. Not even Samantha. My emotions have been all over the place. I just lay in Evan's arms and cry. He tries to soothe me and make me feel better. I want to tell him everything. About Jake. About the baby. I just can't bring myself to do it. I wouldn't even know how to put the words together. What would I say? I'm pregnant and I don't know if it's yours? The thought breaks my heart and I cry even more.

After a while of crying, I fell asleep. Evan has covered me up. I sleep hard and dreamless. It is morning by the time I wake up. Evan has made me breakfast. He hands me a cup of coffee, "So, you want to tell me what's going on?" he asks. I take a deep breath and look at him. I'm shaking and my nerves are getting the best of me. I have to tell him.

"I fought with Samantha. It turned ugly," I say, pushing eggs around my plate. I hear my phone chime in the other room, but I ignore it. "I'm sorry baby," he says. He squeezes my hand. I might as well just tell him about the pregnancy. I would rather him find out from me than anyone else. Sooner or later it's going to come out, I will start showing soon. "There is something else," I say. I shove some eggs in my mouth to buy myself some time. "What is it?" He asks. I swallow hard. I'm just going to say, "Evan, I'm pregnant."

At first, he seems puzzled. I'm holding my breath. "Honey?" I ask. "That explains the pickle jar in your bag," he says, smiling. I laugh and blush. He kisses me and hugs me. He is so excited. "I love you," he says. "I love you, honey," I say. I feel guilty because it may not be his. It breaks my heart that it might not be, but he is so happy, I go against telling him.

I go back to Evan's room to get my bag and check my phone. I have six missed calls and 12 text messages from Jake. "I'll pick you up for the rehearsal dinner," Evan says, kissing me, tears streaming down his face. I kiss him goodbye and walk to my car. Just before I get in, he yells over to me, "I'm going to be a dad!" I wave and smile and get in my car. I can't take this away from him. I know it's wrong to keep Jake in the dark. For now, that's what I am going to do.

I'm walking through the house, and Jake yanks me into the kitchen. He checks to make sure no one is around, "Samantha says you are pregnant."

"I am."

"Is it mine?"

"I have no idea."

"You couldn't tell me?"

"What was I supposed to say? Hey, I'm growing a human who may or may not belong to you?"

"You and Evan have been sleeping together?"

"You know we have. He is my boyfriend after all."

"Well, you are going to have to find out."

"I don't have to do anything."

"Lottie."

There is pain on his face. "Look, I love you. I was stupid. I should have never done the things I did. I want you. I need you," he says. "I have to get ready," I say and walk off, "Keep your mouth shut, by the way." I am shaking by the time I reach my room. I shower and get ready. I take the pickle jar out of my purse and giggle to myself.

The rehearsal dinner is ok for the most part. Evan is very attentive. He stays close to me and waits on me hand and foot. Momma and Daddy watch us with stars in their eyes. There is a lot of tension between me and Samantha, so I try to stay away from her. Momma acts like a buffer between us when we have to talk to each other.

While everyone is mingling after dinner, I step outside for some air. I need some time alone to think. The amount of love Evan has shown me since I told him makes me happy. It's a love I've never known. It is something that has grown every day. My love for Jake hasn't gone away. I just love him differently.

"Hey," Jake says, walking up behind me. "Hey, what are you doing out here?" I ask. "I should ask you the same thing," he says. We stand in silence, the only thing I can hear is the frogs, and the ice clinking in his glass. He smells like he has been drinking too much. I would probably drink like that just to be around my sister most of the time. "I needed some air. Samantha is a bridezilla tonight," he says. I nod. "When are we going to talk about this Lottie?" he asks.

"I don't think there is anything to talk about. Evan is the father. End of story," I say.

Jake reaches over and touches my belly. His touch sends a spark through me. I put my hands on his hand, and we stood like that for a while. We jump when we hear the door open. Momma pokes her head out, "Lottie, Evan is looking for you." I nod at Jake and walk back in. Momma stands there for a moment. She pats my shoulder and follows me.

~ 20 ~

We are all up with the chickens to get ready for the wedding. I spend the first hour of the day laying on the bathroom floor. Morning sickness will be the death of me. I'm almost certain of it. When the feeling has passed, I peel myself off the floor and manage to shower. Samantha still doesn't want me in the wedding, and I am fine with that. There is still a lot of animosity between us. I'm still going to be there with bells and whistles on and play the supportive sister.

Once breakfast is done, and Momma and Samantha leave for the church, I spend some time with Daddy. We mostly talk about the baby, and the plans Evan has for our future. Daddy gives advice the way Momma does, but he always lets me find my way. Whatever decision I make he will always be supportive. "I love you, Daddy," I say, kissing him on the cheek. "I love you, too sugar," he replies. I head upstairs to get ready.

I hear my phone go off just as I'm getting in the shower. I look at my phone and see a message from Jake.

J: I don't know if I want to go through with this.

L: It's your wedding day. You have cold feet. You will be alright.

I finished getting ready and headed down to the kitchen. Daddy finished his coffee and giggled at me for putting a jar of pickles in my purse. "What, I need a snack," I say, "You need to get to the church. You have to get dressed." He puts his coffee cup in the sink then hugs me. "You look beautiful sugar," he says. I blush and sit in the living room waiting for Evan. He refuses to let me drive. I hate driving anyway, so I let him cart me around to places I need to go.

"You are stunning," he says, taking my hand and helping me down the stairs. Heels might not have been a good idea. "Let's ride, Clyde," I say. We head towards the church. This might be one of the hardest things to do. Well, not the hardest. The hardest thing was losing Nina. We arrive at the church and there is already a crowd. Typical Samantha. She invited anyone and everyone. It looks like a circus to me.

Evan finds Daddy, and I head to the bridal room. As much as my sister grates my nerves, she does look beautiful. We take obligatory photos and go through the motions. "I think you are beautiful. I'm sorry for everything," I say. "It's ok. We are sisters. We are supposed to hate each other now and again. I do love you," she says. I tell her I love her, and I head to find Evan.

The sanctuary is full of flowers and balloons, it looks like a kid's birthday party and a funeral all rolled up into one. Despite this, it is pretty. We take our seats and wait for the ceremony to begin. I hate that I'm not standing up there with her, but also glad I'm not. These heels are killing my feet and I'm not even standing.

The music starts to play, and Evan takes my hand and squeezes it. The look on his face is pure joy and love. I smile and kiss his cheek. The flower girl begins her trip down the aisle, followed by the ring bearer and the bridesmaids. They all look so lovely. The music is pretty, too. It would not have been my choice, but it's fitting for Samantha. Once the wedding party has made their journey and gets settled, the wedding march begins.

Jake walks out to stand next to the preacher, and the back doors open. Samantha is radiant and Daddy looks proud. I have a knot in my stomach. I don't know what Jake is going to do. He has been telling me for days that he has doubts and he doesn't know if he can go through with this. He is in love with me. Tears are flowing all around the sanctuary. My emotions are all over the place. I cannot sit still to save my life.

Samantha reaches the altar, and the preacher proceeds with the nuptials. I hold my breath when he gets to the "I Do's". Jake is shaking at this point. Samantha says her part, then Jake repeats what the preacher is saying. All the sudden, he says, "I'm sorry, I can't do this."

There is a silence in the room that is deafening. There are a few murmurs. Samantha is standing frozen, not comprehending what is going on. I'm sitting there with my mouth hanging open. "What do you mean you can't do this?" Samantha asks Jake.

"I'm sorry," Jake says and walks down the aisle out of the sanctuary. His mom gets up and follows him out. After a few minutes of standing in shock, she runs off to the bridal suite. I get up and tell Evan to wait right where he is, and Momma and I go after her. Samantha is in tears and right-fully so. Her soon-to-be husband just walked out on her. I know the reason why, but I dare not say. I know what is about to happen and the thought makes me want to puke.

Momma does her best to console Samantha. I sit in si-lence. I'm not usually good at these kinds of things. I just sit and hold her hand. Daddy knocks on the door, and Jake enters after him. We all are staring at him. There is fear in my eyes. "Maybe we should go and let them have a few mo-ments together," I say, getting up and heading toward the door. "No," Samantha says, "He can tell all of us. He owes us that much."

"Samuel, let everyone know that they can go ahead and head to the fellowship hall. They are welcome to eat. We don't want all that food to go to waste," Momma says to Daddy. Daddy kisses Samantha's cheek and heads to the sanc-tuary. "I think you owe an explanation Jake," Samantha says. She stands up, tall and regal. I admire her. She is trying to save what dignity she has left, after being left at the altar.

"It's been a wonderful six months, Samantha. It has. I've been trying to find a way to say this. It's not you. It's never been you," he says. Tears are streaming down Saman-tha's face. "Then who is it? Who are you so stuck on, that you can't marry me? I thought you loved me." Samantha says. She is shaking with anger but trying to keep her cool. She is trying not to hit him. "I do, but it's just not the right kind of love," Jake says. I'm standing behind him with my hand on the door ready to bolt. I know it's coming. "I'm in love with my ex-girlfriend. It's always been her," Jake says. He turns around and reaches for my hand. "Her? That's your ex?" Samantha yells. The urge to throw up hits me, and I run out the door. I can hear Samantha screaming.

This is the worst day ever. I was hoping he would go through with it. I wanted him too. I know that is probably wrong. It's the truth. I wanted him to get married and leave me alone despite the feelings I have for him. I love Evan, but I love Jake too. It's a disaster. When the screaming stops, I make my way cautiously down to the fellowship hall. I am looking for Evan. Jake grabs me and pulls me into the kitchen. "I really shouldn't be talking to you. I'm looking for Evan, have you seen him?" I ask. "No. I haven't. Lottie, I need to talk to you. I want to be with you," he says.

"I don't have time for this. I want to go home."

"I just left your sister, at the altar no less, and you want to go home?"

"Jake."

"Lottie."

He kisses me. Hard. I try to push him away. This is not the time or the place. I walk out of the kitchen and head toward the front door. I spotted Samantha headed straight for me. Before I can reach the door, she intercepts me and pushes me. "Hey watch it, I'm pregnant," I say. "That's the only reason you are still alive at this point because I want to murder you right now," she says. She pulls me by my arm into the preacher's office and shuts the door, "I want to know what the hell is going on. Right now." I take a deep breath.

"Jake and I were together for a year. I left him because he didn't want a future with me. I also caught him cheating on me with his assistant. I didn't know that he started dating you, much less asked you to be his wife, until he showed up at the BBQ."

"What else. I know there is more. There has to be."

"We spent some time together, while you were running around doing wedding stuff."

I put my hands around my belly. It's more of a protection move than anything. "We also slept together." I take a step back. She has this calm look on her face. It's scary. I don't know what she is going to do. I take another step back. "Is he the father of your child?" she asks.

"I don't know."

"You don't know?"

"I don't know. It could be his. It could be Evan's.

"That's classy Lottie."

She marches off to God knows where and I rush outside. I forgot my purse, so I run back in to grab it. Momma and Daddy are standing outside when I finally get out of the building. I tell them I'm leaving to go home. Jake is standing with his parents and sees me walking across the parking lot. He heads towards me. "Not now Jake, please not now," I say. He stops beside me. Suddenly, the doors of the church are kicked open. It's Evan and he is pissed. He makes a bee-line straight for us. Everything is moving in slow motion. As soon as Evan reaches us, he throws a punch and hits Jake in the face, "You son of a bitch!" Blood starts flowing from his nose and he hits the ground. "Oh my god," I say. I grab an old shirt from the car and bend down and place it on his face to try and stop the bleeding. Daddy and my cousin get to Evan and try to keep hold of him back before he can do more damage.

Evan looks at me with disgust. That hurts more than anything. I get in the car and drove nowhere in particular. I have so many thoughts in my head. My relationship is over with Evan, this much is true. I want to talk to him though. I need to explain things. After a few hours, I pulled up to the house. I go to my room and lock the door, turning my phone off. I lay down. I think.

~ 21 ~

These past three months have been hard. I haven't spoken to Evan at all. He refuses to speak to me now. Duke says to give him some time. I have ignored Jake completely. Samantha will not speak to me and wants nothing to do with me. I quit the bar and took up a job at the cafe. It would have been too hard and too much of a conflict of interest. There are more hours, and I am making more money. My days have been filled with work and doctors' appointments. Nothing more than that.

I am headed home from work. My back is killing me, and my feet hurt. On a whim, I sent him a text.

L: Hey. Can we talk?

It's a good four hours before I get a response.

E: Yeah, Come by tomorrow.

L: Ok. I'll be there after work.

The day at the cafe is long. I go over in my mind what to say to Evan. I want to make amends. I don't know if he will take me back. I want him in my life. I love him. I go home and change and shower before I go over. I text him to let him know I am on the way.

Evan is waiting on the porch when I get there. He has two glasses of sweet tea sitting out. How thoughtful. I take it as a good sign. I pull up and park, and he walks to my car. My nerves are haywire at this point. I have no idea how this is going to go. I take a deep breath. I start to speak, but Evan pulls me into a hug. We stand like this for what seems like forever. I miss his arms being around me. He places a hand on my stomach and then takes my hand.

We walk hand in hand to the porch, and I take a seat. My mouth is dry, and I drink my tea quickly. Evan just smiles and fills my tea back up. "Want some pickles?" he asks. I just laugh and he brings some out. "So, what do you want to talk to me about?" he says, after taking a sip of his tea. I start with small talk. I ask how he has been, and how Duke is.

We sit in silence for a good bit. The sun is starting to set. Evan reaches over and takes my hand. "I've been thinking a lot about things," he says.

"About?"

"Us. The baby."

"Tell me."

"I want to see where this goes. I still love you. I always will. I want to know if the baby is mine."

"Ok. We can do that."

"Why didn't you tell me about Jake?"

"It was a very delicate time with the wedding and every-thing. I was drunk. He was drunk. There was a history. It hap-pened. I am very sorry. About everything."

Evan is staring at the floor. He looks like he is lost in thought. I know it's not the best apology, but it's what I have. I understand if this doesn't go anywhere. "We all make mis-takes," he says after a few minutes, "I forgive you. We will take this slow." I sigh with relief. Now the ball is in my court. If it is Evan's baby, then I will be with him. If it's Jake's, I would have to build a relationship with him. I love Jake, so it's possible. I love Evan even more.

I feel better by the time I leave Evan's house. I think things are starting to look up. Momma is in the living room when I get home. "Come sit with me, child," she says. I curl up on the couch with her. My Momma has been the best through all of this. She knows I'm struggling. We talked for a while.

"I think I want to have a prenatal paternity test," I say, "I don't want to wait five months to find out." Momma starts to rub my feet. It feels good. "I think that would be a good thing to do. We can call the doctor and set it up," she says. I go upstairs and get ready for bed. I hope that this will settle things once and for all. I know what I want, but I know that whatever happens, I have to deal with it. Either way, it's fate.

I know I have to tell Jake what I'm going to do. I've been avoiding him like the plague. It's late, but I know he is awake. I text him. After a few minutes, my phone rings. "I was won-dering if you were ever going to answer your phone," he says. "I know," I replied. I ask him how he is if he has heard from Samantha, about his parents. I'm not nearly as nervous as when I was talking to Evan about everything. "I am going to have a paternity test done. It's a prenatal one. So, you and Evan will have to give samples. I'm calling the doctor tomorrow to set everything up," I say. Jake wants to know what will happen if the baby is his.

"Let's just find out who the father is first," I tell him. We say our goodbyes, and I try to sleep. I am a little restless. I like being in control of things, but leaving it up to fate is hard,

We are meeting at the hospital for prenatal testing. We haven't been in the same room since the wedding. The tension is unbearable. Evan is holding my hand while we sit in silence. Jake can't sit still. Momma is here with us and is acting as a buffer. The nurse calls both men back one at a time. I am getting more nervous as time passes.

Once Evan and Jake are done giving their samples, it's time for me to go back. Jake leaves to go to the cafeteria to get some coffee. He doesn't want to be in the same room as Evan. It would be a disaster. Momma and I sit in the little room for a bit before the nurse comes back. I see the size of the needle and I immediately feel sick to my stomach. I'm hoping this isn't going to hurt even though the nurse assures me. She says I will feel a lot of pressure. The doctor comes in and starts the task at hand. Momma holds my hand as the doctor and nurse complete the procedure. The results will take about two weeks to come back.

It wasn't as bad as I thought it was going to be. "Can I talk to you, Lottie?" Jake asks, "alone?" I nod at Momma and Evan to let them know it's ok, that I will only be a minute. "What is it?" I ask. I'm slightly annoyed as I desperately need a nap and a back rub. "Have you thought about what you are going to do once the baby is here?" He asks.

"No, I haven't."

"Don't you think you need to make a decision?"

"Don't you think pressuring me is a little wrong?

"I'm not trying to pressure you, Lottie."

"Look, when the results come back, we will go from there. Right now, I'm trying to repair things with Evan."

Jake has an annoyed look on his face, but it is what it is. He just has to be patient. This is a big deal for all of us. I know he wants to be together. I don't know if I can bring myself to have that with him. I know that I haven't been the best person in the world. I've made mistakes, too. We could be what we once were. We would have to build from the ground up, just like Evan and I are doing.

Before I leave the nurse gives Momma an envelope that contains the sex of the baby is. We are having a party on Sunday. I was against having a gender reveal, but for the sake of my Momma, I let her host one. So, I let her. Momma has gone all out since she found out I was pregnant. The guest room is full of everything I need for a baby. She is so excited and proud. Judging by everything, she is going to spoil the baby rotten and I'm ok with that.

The week has dragged on. When Sunday arrives, I am exhausted. I had no idea that growing a human would be this much work. Some women make it look so damn easy, but for me, it's like juggling chainsaws. The cravings, the morning sickness, my swollen ankles. After breakfast, I lay down to take a nap before the party. Momma has the house decorated with balloons and streamers, and she ordered a special cake. Friends and family have shown up. We are all sitting around outside talking and watching the kids play when a car pulls into the drive.

Samantha gets out of her car and is carrying a few gift bags and balloons. She is the one person I didn't think would come. We sent her an invitation, even though I was quite sure that she was still angry with me. I get up and walk over to her and she hugs me tight. "Let's talk after the party," she says. I nod and we walk over to everyone. It's time to cut the cake and see if I am having a boy or a girl. I am slightly nervous, but I will be happy either way.

Everyone gathers around and I cut the cake. The cake is blue. I am having a little boy. Tears start streaming down my face. I am so happy at this moment surrounded by my family and friends. I only wish we knew who the father was, so he can be here to share this moment. We still have a week to go before we find out.

The party is over by five o'clock. I decided to take a piece of cake to Evan and Duke. I haven't been to the bar in a while. I see Duke at the bar as I walk in and show him the cake. He points to the office where Evan is. "Hey beautiful," he says as I walk in. He kisses my belly and then kisses me. It's a sweet gesture. He grabs a plastic fork and digs in. I tell him about the party and about Samantha coming. He thinks it's a good idea that we talk.

Samantha is in the kitchen when I get home, cleaning up some dishes from the party. "I was wondering when you were going to get back," she says. I pick up a towel and start drying dishes as she washes them. "Why Momma wanted to use real dishes, I will never know," I say. We both laugh. We talk about odds and ends as if she is trying to avoid why she wanted to talk to me. After we are done, we sit at the table and drink some tea. "I didn't think you would show up," I say.

"Well, you are having my nephew. I'm going to spoil that little boy. I also wanted to make up."

"Really?"

"Yeah. I've been giving it a lot of thought here lately. I want to be sisters again."

"We can do that."

"I want to say I'm sorry for the way I acted, too. I was crazy. I could have handled it a different way. I was so angry I wanted to get back at you, so I told Evan."

"You had a right to be angry. It was a whole clusterfuck."

"Jake and I had it out about a week after what happened. I still don't forgive him."

I told Samantha about what happened between me and Jake. I told her about Sarah, and not wanting to settle down with me. The only thing I can come up with is that he was only settling down because that is what his mother wanted. Poor Samantha just went along with it, in the belief that Jake did love her. I think he does, but not in the capacity to marry. "Do you think the baby belongs to Jake?" She asks me. "I am not sure. I think it's Evan's, but there is that small chance that it does belong to Jake," I say.

We finish our cups of tea and turn in for the night. Samantha is going to stay for a few days, which is nice. I hope we can spend some time together while she is here.

~ 23 ~

I've given a lot of thought to the job offer with the museum. I want to take the job, but with only 3 months left till the birth, it wouldn't make sense to work for three months and then go on maternity leave. I called Mr. Wilton and let him know the decision I have made. He says that my position will be open when I am ready. I plan to move to Chattanooga in 6 months. The thought scares me, knowing that I will have a newborn. I won't know anyone so it will be hard to have someone keep the baby.

Momma and Samantha both say that they can take turns to help. I know it won't be a problem for Momma, but with Samantha's public relations firm taking off she may not have time. I keep the offer in the back of my mind though. The thought of me possibly being a single mom scares me. If the baby is Jake's, he will be in his life, but I don't think I would ever consider another romantic relationship with Jake. I have no idea where mine and Evan's relationship is heading.

I put in my two weeks at the café. I have enough money saved up, and work is becoming a chore. I stepped outside to take a break and checked my phone. I have a missed call from the doctor's office. They called to tell me the results were in. I have a wide range of emotions at this point. I have an appointment tomorrow anyway, so I plan on picking up the results then. I spent the evening with the family. "What are you going to do with the results," Momma asks, shuffling a deck of cards. "I don't know," I say. We start playing spades, but my mind is somewhere else. What do I do with the results? Should I tell the father immediately? Should I keep them 'til the baby is born? I'm not sure. I have a lot of excitement, but I also have a lot of dread.

I got to see an ultrasound today of my baby boy. It's been a while since my last one. He is growing and measuring ahead of schedule. He is so beautiful. I can't wait to hold him in my arms and hear him cry for the first time. The doctor decides that he wants to induce me if I don't go into labor first. The nurse gives me the DNA results, but I wait to open it.

When I get back in the car, I stare at the envelope. I'm nervous. I'm scared. I hope the one person I want to be the father, is the father. I'm shaking as I open the envelope. I read through the letter, and at the end, is the result. I cry. I cry because I am happy. I cry because the wait is over. I cry because now maybe, I can have a complete family. I know what I have to do. I make a plan and head home.

I wrap up my last day at the café. It's bitter-sweet. . Momma, Samantha, and I spend our days shopping for the baby and spending time together. Daddy is taking it in stride. He has been a trooper with everything. He has built a crib for his new grandson, and it is so beautiful. Momma has converted the guest room into a nursery. They are both so proud. I've been spending a lot of time with Evan.

Evan and my relationship are growing despite everything. I can't help but love him. He has been so patient and kind. He has been amazing through these last few months of the pregnancy. He has been very attentive. Duke doesn't like the fact that Evan and I have been spending a lot of time together. I hope that he will come around.

~ 24 ~

It's been two months since I got the results of the DNA test. I know I shouldn't have held on to it, but I did. However, I wanted to make sure I was positive about what I was doing. I call Jake to tell him I'm coming to Birmingham tomorrow, that I need to speak to him. This is something that needs to be done in person, and not over the phone. For the first time in months, I slept peacefully. I am no longer on edge. After breakfast, Daddy offers to drive me down, but this is something I need to do on my own. I know he means well; he just wants to protect me.

The trip down to Birmingham is a nice one. It's a gorgeous day with a cloudless sky. I decided to stop by Nina's grave. I haven't been here since she passed. I placed a bouquet of her favorite flowers on her headstone. I tell her everything. I know that she would be proud of me. She would give me her advice. She would hug me and tell me everything will be ok in the end. I wish she would be able to meet my little one. She would love him as much as I do. I feel something that might be a contraction, but I ignore it. I sit for a bit before I leave the cemetery.

I met Jake at the Indian restaurant that we had our first lunch date at. "You are glowing," he says as he walks up to my car. He helps me out and we head into the restaurant. I've been craving curry and I'm a little excited about it. After we order our food, we make a little small talk. I haven't seen him since the doctor's visit. We are both nervous as he knows why I'm here. I get uncomfortable as another contraction hits. I ignore it again, thinking it's Braxton Hicks. "So, what did you want to talk to me about?" he asked me.

I try to beat around the bush, but there is no use. "I have the results," I say. He is a little upset that I haven't told him sooner, but I decided to wait. He puts his fork down and gives me his full attention. My nerves are getting the best of me. I take a sip of water. Just as I am about to tell him the results, I feel a pop and dampness. "Well, spit it out Lottie," he says. "I can't. My water just broke," I say. Another strong contraction hits and it is unbearable. This pain is something else. Jake jumps up and helps me out of the seat, "We have to get you to the hospital." The owner comes out and Jake lets her know what's going on, and he will be back later to settle the check.

I call Momma and tell her I'm in labor. She and Daddy leave immediately. The drive to the hospital is a short one, but it feels like it's thirty thousand miles away. The contractions are getting stronger and closer together. I hope we make it before the baby comes. I do not want to have this kid on the side of the highway. We make it to the hospital, and they rush me back to labor and delivery. It's going to be at least three hours before Momma and Daddy get here. I can't reach Samantha. So, the only other person here is Jake. This is not how I planned it.

Everything is happening so fast. By the time we get back to the room, I am dilated to a ten and it's time to push. It hurts so bad. We didn't have time for an epidural. Jake holds my hand and talks me through everything. I'm pretty sure I broke his hand. One more final push and my baby boy makes his way into the world. He is gorgeous. I'm exhausted.

I'm asleep by the time Momma and Daddy arrive. Evan comes into the room, too. I guess Daddy called him after I called. Samantha gets there about an hour later. When I wake, Momma is the only one in the room. Momma is holding the baby. She puts him in my arms, and I am so in love. He has ten perfect fingers and ten perfect toes. He is the spitting image of me. Momma goes and gets everyone.

When everyone comes in, there are tears of joy. "Everyone meet Jackson Everett," I say. Everyone takes turns holding Jackson. I realize I didn't get to tell Jake or Evan the results. I guess now is a good time. "Can I speak to Evan and Jake alone, please?" I ask. Momma and Daddy hug me and kiss the baby and go down to the cafeteria. Samantha doesn't want to leave me alone, but I tell her it's ok. Everything will be fine.

I didn't plan to tell them both in the same room, but thanks to Jackson's determination to enter the world, it's something I just have to go through with. "I wanted to tell you guys separately who the father is, but Jackson had other plans," I say, smiling down at him. "I sat on the results for a long time 'til I was sure of what to do. I know that it has been nerve-wracking to you both, and for that, I am sorry," I say. Evan sits down in the chair across the room. Jake remains standing by the window. "I want you to know that either way, each one of you means a lot to me, and I thank you for being a part of my life in different ways," I say, soothing Jackson as he starts to cry. I know I'm stalling. I am trying to find the words. I don't know what the reaction will be. I just know that there is a lot of love here.

We have been home from the hospital for a few weeks now. Evan has been the best father. He is here more than he is at home, except for the bar. He holds Jackson and just stares in awe. For the first time in a very long time, I am truly happy. I have gone through every storm that has come my way, and now I have my little family. Watching Momma and Daddy with Jackson is a wonderful sight to see. Duke has come around more. He loves Jackson and he is happy for Evan and me.

Evan wants to have dinner to celebrate the birth of our child. This is the first time we will be alone since Jackson has arrived. I get ready for our date, and Evan picks me up around four o'clock in the afternoon. "You look so beautiful," he says, hugging me tightly. "I try," I say, laughing. We drive through town past the diner, and into the other side of town. "Where are we going?" I ask, kind of confused because we just passed the restaurant. "I have a surprise for you," he says. He takes my hand and squeezes it.

We pull into the driveway of a quaint little house. It's a cute little three-bedroom brick house with a bright red tin roof. I've seen it before, but not like this. This is the old Mc-

Callister place. It looks like it's been fixed up. "What's this?" I ask. "It's your surprise. This is our home. I've spent the past few weeks fixing it up. I originally bought it for me because it was time for me to kind of move out of Dad's and into my own space. Since Jackson was born and I'm the father, it's our place now," he says. Tears well up in my eyes.

I hug Evan. "This is the best surprise ever," I say. "Come on, let's go inside," he says and takes my hand. The inside is beautiful. It has an open living room and kitchen, with a sprawling back porch. "We can put up a fence out here. Maybe get a dog. There are new cabinets, and the bathroom has been redone. The floor is walnut," he says, giving me a tour of our new home.

I walk to the window and look out across the backyard. I imagine a playset for Jackson. Maybe a pool. A large garden. It all seems so real. I have never in my life been so happy. "Lottie," Evan says. "I turn around and look at him. "Will you marry me?" he asks.

"What?"

"Will you marry me?"

"Oh my god."

Evan pulls a ring box from his pocket and hits one knee. "You're the one for me. Since we were kids, I've always loved you. Since you came into my life, I have been a better man. Now, we have Jackson, and I want to be the best father to him, and the best man I can for you," he says. I see a tear stream down his face. "Yes. Yes. Yes," I scream. I run over to him and he puts the ring on my finger. We hug and kiss and hold each other. I'm so happy.

When we walk out of the house, everyone is here. Momma, Daddy, Samantha, Duke, and Jackson have all come to share this wonderful moment. At this moment, I am truly blessed. Looking around and seeing my family's happiness, smiles, and tears of joy, I realize that this is what my heart needed. This my friends is my happily ever after.

~ 25 ~

Epilogue

Jackson is growing so fast. He has the best personality. He loves animals, tractors, trucks, and cows, and he is all boy. My beautiful blue-eyed boy. The day is gorgeous, and the sun is shining bright. I watch Evan and Jackson playing in the backyard with our dog. Today he turns two. The first year of his life was a little rough. He had some lung issues and spent time in the hospital. You wouldn't be able to tell now, he is so full of life. He has the kindest heart and an old soul.

Evan is running the Broken Wagon Saloon full time now that Duke has retired. Duke spends his days working the farm with Daddy, and spending time with Jackson. Momma has been a big help with Jackson. She keeps him when Evan and I work. She loves him and spoils him rotten. She is the best Nana to Jackson, and for that I am thankful.

Samantha's public relations firm took off the year that Jackson was born. Now, she is one of the largest firms in Alabama and serves the surrounding states. We are all so proud of her. She comes home when she can, and we enjoy visiting her. Our relationship has grown, and we are closer. She loves Jackson and is the best Auntie Sam.

As for me, I decided not to take the job in Chattanooga. I wanted to stay here, for us to be close to family. I opened a small art studio in town. Kids of all ages come in and paint whatever their heart desires. We also offer Sips and Paint for adults. The studio is doing well. I think about Nina often, and I know she is with me always.

It's weird to me that my life has turned into something that I never thought would happen. I am married, with a son and a wonderful husband. I never knew what real love was till Evan. This is exactly where I am meant to be.

Acknowledgements

I had this crazy idea one day when I woke up that I was going to finally write a book. Here it is. There are a few people I would like to thank for sticking by me through all sorts of things. First and foremost, my husband Andy, who is always up for my crazy adventures. He believes in me when no one else will. To my family, Momma, Adam, and Valerie, whom I love very much. To Jennie Banks, my friend and Editor. You took on this crazy thing and helped me make it the best I could. To my book bestie and beta reader, Amber Beardsley, thank you for sharing my love of books. To my best friend Ericka Benavides, thank you for being on my side.

About The Author

Ashlea Thompson was born and raised in beautiful Alabama. Ashlea loves her family and they are the most important thing to her. When she is not working, she spends her time with her wonderful husband Andy, going on crazy adventures. She also loves to spend time with her fur babies Beau Dean and Bama Jean. She is an avid reader and a lover of Atlanta Braves Baseball and Crimson Tide Football. She is also a member of the Alabama Writer's Co-operative. She currently resides in Albertville, AL.

Continue reading for a sneak peek!

Make You Love Me

By Ashlea Thompson

Coming this Winter!

1.
Detective Alex McGuire

I am startled awake by the sound of the phone ringing. It's three o'clock in the morning. I feel like I just got to sleep. I fumble around for the lamp, nearly knocking everything off my bedside table. "Sara, you better have a good reason to call this early in the damn morning," I say, "A body has been discovered at Cane's creek. You might as well get up and get down here. It's a doozy," Sara says. I sigh and tell her I'll be down there in about an hour.

I sit on the side of the bed for a moment. I've seen a lot of murder cases over my time as a detective. Fifteen years on the job, and it still gets me every time. I look over at Vivian, sound asleep. I don't want to wake her; she has been exhausted from her job as a nurse. I get dressed and make my way into the kitchen. I make some coffee and leave a note for Vivian. It's tranquil when I step outside. Vivan and I chose this neighborhood due to the location, with access to good schools, and we aren't far from the city. Luthersville is a bustling city. The crime rate isn't high, and most cases are closed quickly. We haven't had a murder in a while.

When I arrive at Cane's Creek, there are several patrol cars. Officers have cordoned off the area. I take a deep breath and make my way up to the scene. The officer lets me through, and I find Sara. "What do we know?" I ask. She motions me to follow her. "We have what appears to be a twenty-one-year-old white female, about 5'6. Her face had been beaten. The coroner is still working on her now," she says. We reach the bank of the creek and the body. The scene is gruesome, and the smell is atrocious. "What are we looking at here, Doc?"

I ask. Dr. Kenneth Mashburn has worked on several cases with me over the years. "It's not good, Detective. It looks like the cause of death is asphyxiation. We will know more when the autopsy is completed. We aren't sure who she is. We will request dental records. It may be the girl missing last month, but we don't know for sure at this point," he says. Marie Stevens is a woman who was abducted in the middle of the night three weeks ago. Her case has not been solved yet, and her parents have done everything to bring her home safely. Hopefully, if this is Marie, we can bring some closure. "Why don't we get some samples from her father or mother and see what we come up with before we do that. Dental records can take eight weeks. I don't want to wait that long. I will make the call and go see them this morning," I say.

Kenneth calls me back over and points to her chest. "It looks like some kind of wound." I bend down and study the wound. The shape looks like some kind of crosshair symbol, placed right where the heart would be located. "What could have caused this?" I ask Kenneth. He stands and thinks for a few minutes. "It doesn't look like it's been carved. It looks more like a burn. Like a brand," he says. I stand back up and motion for Sara to come over. I fill her in on what we have found. "Make sure the techs comb the area. Anything that looks suspicious bag it and tag it," I say. Sara nods and goes to give the orders to the crime unit. I write down all the information that Kenneth has given me. It looks like it's going to be a long day.

By the time I leave the scene, it's too late to go back home to have coffee with Vivian before she heads to work. I decided to go to the office and get started on the day. I have a mountain of paperwork to go through, and now I have this case to get started on. I shoot a text to Vivian and then set to work. I make a few phone calls and wait for Kenneth to call me with a report. I call Marie's parents. They have agreed to meet with me today. I hate having to have these conversations with victims' families. It never gets easier. Sara comes in at about a quarter past eight. "I have some news. I got the autopsy report from Kenneth," She says, taking a seat in front of me. I lean forward and wait for her to tell me what was found. "Doc says she has been dead for about three days. She died of blunt force trauma to the back of the head. He believes the killer stabbed her for good measure. The wound on her chest was made with a home-made branding iron. I have reason to believe it was made with a coat hanger. Traces of coating were found in the wound," She says. "Ok. I am going over to the Stevens residence around ten to get some samples. Wanna come with me?" I ask her. We swing by the coffee shop on the way to the Stevens' house.

The Stevens lived just north of the city in a sprawling neighborhood known for their large houses and rolling green lawns. The residences in this are primarily doctors, bankers, and the business elite. The crime rate is surprisingly low, and there have not been any significant issues here. The house is a large two-story home with a three-car garage and a large backyard. Mr. Stevens is a businessman who owns a brokerage firm. Mrs. Stevens works for local charities. From what I understand, Marie Stevens is an only child and graduated top of her class. She got into Harvard and was to study law. She was an outgoing individual who loved her friends and her family. The night she was abducted, she was walking home from the country club about three blocks away. There had been a party for the young adults of the community. Marie opted to walk home from the party, as opposed to having someone take her home. We aren't sure if she was specifically targeted or not. If the body found is Marie Stevens, we will start working on finding who committed the crime.

Sara is nervous. This is the first time she has worked a homicide. Honestly, there hasn't been a homicide in Luthersville in ten years. Sara has only been my partner for the past five years. "Don't be nervous. I'll do most of the talking. You can take the samples," I say to her. She nods and knocks on the door. The Stevens' maid answers the door. "My name is Detective McGuire, and this is Sara, my partner. Mr. and Mrs. Stevens are expecting us," I say, producing my badge and I.D. "Right this way," the maid says and motions us to follow her. The house is decorated mainly in white. There are few pops of color here and there. The hallway leading to the living room is full of family photos. There are pictures of Maire in various stages of life. She is a gorgeous young woman.

"Good morning, detectives," Mrs. Stevens says as she enters the room, "Come on over and have a seat. Lorraine, can you please bring our guests some tea?" Lorraine disappears and comes back five minutes later with a tray of glasses and a pitcher. She doesn't speak as she serves our drinks. I find it a bit odd. "Thank you for seeing us today. We have some news on your daughter's disappearance," I say. Mrs. Stevens takes a sip of her tea. "Can we wait for my husband? He should be home any minute. I called him after I spoke to you this morning," She says. She looks very calm right now. In the time I have known her, she has always kept composure. I would be a raving mess. I know Vivian would be too if it were her. We made some small talk about the weather and her various charities. Mr. Stevens arrives about an hour later.

"I'm sorry to keep you guys waiting. I tried to leave the office as soon as I could," he says. He shakes our hands as we exchange pleasantries. We all take a seat and get down to the matter at hand. "At three o'clock this morning, a body was discovered at Cane's Creek. We have reasons to believe this may be your missing daughter. At this point, we are looking at all possibilities. Since your daughter's case has no new information, we want to check and see if we can identify her. We thought it might be quicker to use DNA samples to identify the body. Will you two be willing to submit to a DNA swab?" I say. Mr. and Mrs. Stevens looked at each other and then back at me. "I guess it wouldn't hurt," Mr. Stevens says. "Great, Sara here will be taking the samples, and we will submit them to our lab. We should know if it is a match within the next twenty-four hours. We will let you know the results," I say. Sara stands and begins taking swabs from the mouth of each of them. When we are done, we say our goodbyes. I leave my card with them and let them know that I will call soon.

When we reach the office, I have a note from Kenneth to call him as soon as possible. When I get settled into my office, I call him right away. "Detective. I have some information for you. The cause of death is confirmed. It was asphyxiation second to overdose. We found large amounts of Midazolam in her system," he says. I think for a moment. "So whoever he is, he kept her sedated?" I ask. "Heavily. I took samples to compare DNA. I've sent them to the lab," he responds. "Ok, good. Sara turned the samples from the Stevens in about an hour ago. Hopefully, we will hear back something this afternoon or in the morning," I say. We hung up the phone. I decided to go and take a look at the evidence we have from the beginning. I want to refresh my memory with the information if the results come back positive.

I spend most of the afternoon going through evidence. I made a list of people Marie had been around. I make a plan to talk to the individuals and see if they know any more information. I want to find Marie's killer more than anything now. Seeing the poor girl's body has ignited a fire in me. I am going to do everything possible to solve this case. It's late when I finally leave the office. I hope and pray I can have a whole night of sleep. I have a feeling I am going to need it. Vivian is home when I arrive, and I heat my dinner in the microwave. We sat and talked about the case. I usually don't do that, but I need someone to bounce theories off someone other than Sara. "I just can't imagine. Do you think it's the missing girl?" she asks, sipping on her tea. I shake my head as I put a bite of food in my mouth. "For the family's sake, I hope it is. They need closure. It will be difficult, but there will be peace in it," I say. Vivian shakes her head. We finish up dinner and tea and then head to bed.

"I got some information for you, boss," Kenneth says, standing at the door. I call Sara, and we meet in the conference room. I have most of the information on the open kidnapping case spread out on the table. There isn't much. "Lay it on me, I say. "We don't have the DNA samples back yet. We should have those this afternoon. We found some trace evidence on Miss Steven's body. It's male. The lab is running it through the system now to see if we get a hit. Upon further investigation, we found that Miss Stevens was raped. Several times. There is a lot of scarring. We also found several scars that look like she may have been tortured," he says, handing over the reports. I scan the reports briefly. I have a feeling this is one sick person we have on our hands. "Put a rush on those results. The sooner, the better," I say.

The results came in around four-thirty in the afternoon. I was just about to leave for the day and head home. I take a look and print the report out. It is Marie Stevens. This sends a series of shivers down my spine. It's a relief that we have found her, though a tragedy that we found her dead. It will not be an easy task to deliver this news to her parents. This is the first in a series of breaks that will come later. The next step is to comb through witnesses and people at the party. I am hoping to find out what happened and piece it together. There is no way to disappear without someone noticing. I called Sara and let her know. We decided to go ahead and tell her parents. Sara meets me at the Stevens home.

When I knock on the door, Mr. Stevens answers the door. "Detectives, we are having supper. What is this about?" he asks. "We have information about your daughter. I apologize for not calling. This is urgent," I responded. We stand there for a moment before he invites us in. We make our way to the dining room. I feel bad for interrupting their dinner. "I apologize for interrupting, but we have the DNA test back," Sara says. The color has drained from Mrs. Stevens' face. "We have confirmed that the body of the young woman found two days ago through DNA testing is that of your daughter, Marie," I say. There is a long silence. Mr. Stevens walks out of the room, and Mrs. Stevens begins to sob. Sara goes over to Mrs. Stevens and consoles her. Mr. Stevens enters the room again. He hugs and holds his wife. I can't imagine what is going through their mind right now. "We will need you to come down to the Medical Examiner's office to identify the body officially," I say. We agree that tomorrow will be fine. I want to give them a chance to be alone and process what we have told them.

The following morning, I met the Stevens at the Examiner's office. I left Sara to sort through and locate individuals to interview. After exchanging pleasantries, we entered the building. Kenneth comes out to greet us. I would be lying if I said this was easy. We enter the morgue, and tears are flowing. My heart hurts for them. Vivian and I don't have children yet, but I know I would be a mess of emotions if it were me. The Stevens family is precisely that.

When we enter the room, the body is laid on a table with a sheet over it. Kenneth thought it would be better than having her in a drawer. We approach the table, and Mrs. Stevens reaches over and holds my hand. I squeeze it to let her know that it's going to be ok and that I am there for them. I nod at Kenneth, and he pulls back the sheet. Mrs. Stevens lets out a sob, and her husband places a hand on her shoulder. "That's her. That is our Marie," he says. "Would you like some time alone?" I ask them. They both nod in agreement. Kenneth and I leave the room.

"I hate this part," Kenneth says. "I know, buddy. This is the biggest murder in years for this city. I want to work hard to find who did this," I say. He pats me on the back, and I head back to the office. Sara has compiled a long list of names at the country club the night of Marie's abduction. We set to work tracking down everyone. By mid-afternoon, we had tracked down about four people. We set off to the country club. Waterford Country Club is a massive resort covering a mass of land featuring a golf course, several pools, tennis courts, ballrooms, and a convention center. It's where the elite and wealthy come to unwind. I never understood why. To me, paying that much money to be a part of an elite club is ridiculous. I flash my badge at the guard hut and pull through the gate. A young woman greets us at the front desk." How can I help you?" she asks. "I'm Detective McGuire, and this is Detective Raines. We are looking for a Raven Devereaux," I say. The young woman speaks into a walkie-talkie. A few minutes later, Raven comes sauntering up to the desk. I introduce ourselves, "Is there somewhere we can speak in private?" I ask.

Raven takes us to a back office. It's small but adequate. "What do you wanna know?" Raven asks, taking a seat in the office chair. Sara and I remain standing. "We want to talk to you about Marie Stevens," I say. Raven has a puzzled look on her face. "She has been missing, right?" She asks.

"Yes. We located Marie's body earlier this week."

"She is dead?"

"Yes."

Tears started trickling down her face. "Do you know what happened?" She asks. "We have reasons to believe she was murdered. We need help to piece together the night she disappeared. Who she was with, what time she left, all of that. We thought you might be able to help us," I say. We let her work out what is happening. After a few minutes, she starts talking. "She was hanging out with a group of people. They were all talking and dancing. A guy walked up to her and asked her to dance. She danced with him, but not for long. She went back to her friends. I didn't see her leave with anyone. She doesn't live far from here, so it's not uncommon for her to walk here. She has a car, but she isn't a fan of being behind the wheel since she wrecked her car a few years ago," she says. I make a mental note. "Do you know what this guy looked like?" I ask. She tilts her head in thought, trying to remember. "He was sort of tall, blonde hair. It kind of had a little bit of a limp, but it wasn't that noticeable. I can't tell you what he was wearing. I think he worked here. I'm not sure if he still does. This is a big place, and they have a lot of staff. A lot of people don't know each other. That's all I can remember," she says. Sara finishes with the notes in her notebook. "Thank you. Here is my card. Call me if you remember anything else," I say, handing her a business card.

We head towards the front of the building. "We need a complete list of employees here. Do you think they have photos of all their employees?" I nod. "It's possible. We will call their Human Resources and see if they can get us all the information," I say. We are directed to the Human Resource department, and we request the information we need. The director thinks she can get the info, but it might take a while to run the report as there are about 200 full-time and part-time employees. I give her Sara's number and tell her to call us when she has everything. The list may help in gaining more information or giving us a possible suspect. "I want to talk to the Stevens again," I say. "You may want to wait a few days. They are laying their daughter to rest this week. Kenneth released the body already," Sara says. The ride back to the office is quiet. I spend the rest of the afternoon doing paperwork before heading home. We have a full day of interviews tomorrow, as most of the individuals Sara contacted are willing to talk to us.